A GIRL AND HER ELEPHANT

A GIRL AND HER ELEPHANT

ZOEY GONG

Red Empress Publishing
www.RedEmpressPublishing.com

Copyright © Zoey Gong
www.ZoeyGong.com

Cover by Cherith Vaughan
www.CoversbyCherith.com

All rights reserved. No part of this publication may be reproduced, stored in a retrieval system, or transmitted in any form or by any means, electronic, mechanical, photocopying, recoding, or otherwise, without the prior written consent of the author.

For all the elephants of Thailand and around the world.

CHAPTER ONE

The cries of the elephant could be heard throughout the jungle.

Kanita could no longer ignore the elephant's suffering. Even though her father—the king's mahout—had warned her to stay away, she had to see what was happening for herself. She snuck out of her bedroom window and ran through the village to the royal stables where the white elephant was in heavy labor.

Even though it was late at night, the stables and yard were lit with torches, and mahouts were running here and there, trying to calm the rest of the elephant herd. But they seemed incapable of being consoled, and each one trumpeted in distress.

"Bring more hot water!" Kanita heard her father call to one of his men. "And my kris. I will have to cut the baby loose."

Her father had asked for his dagger! *The poor elephant*, Kanita thought. If the elephant—one of the sacred white elephants—died, the king would be displeased. She moved a bale of hay to a stable window and climbed on top of it to get a better view.

On the floor of the stables was the large white elephant. She was straining to birth her calf into the world and tears seeped from her eyes.

She looked at Kanita, and Kanita's heart froze in her chest. It was as though she could hear the elephant begging her for help.

The elephant's wet eyes found Kanita's, and she raised her trunk toward her.

Kanita jumped down from the hay bale and ran into the stables. She had to do something to help. As she entered the building, she saw her father walk behind the elephant with his kris.

"Por! No!" Kanita cried as she ran to him, pulling on his arm. "You'll kill her."

"Kanita!" he said sternly. "I told you to stay in the house with your mother. Get out of here."

"No, I can help," she said. She went to the elephant and looked at where the baby was supposed to come out. The area was red and swollen, but she thought she could see a trunk trying to wiggle out.

She had never helped birth a baby elephant before. As a girl, she was forbidden from becoming a mahout. But she had helped her mother bring a woman's baby into the world just a few days before. It didn't look so different to her. She just needed to reach inside and pull the baby out. And with her small hands and arms, she thought she was just the right size to do it.

She slid her hands inside the mother elephant.

"Be careful," her father cautioned. "Can you feel the calf's legs?"

She wasn't sure what she was feeling. It was like nothing

A Girl and Her Elephant

in the world she had touched before. She closed her eyes and let her hands do the seeing for her.

She felt it. The trunk. She could feel the length of it and the ridges up to the baby elephant's face. She felt the trunk wrap around her arm.

"I feel its face!" Kanita cried.

"Keep going," her father said.

She pushed further into the elephant, all the way to her shoulders. She slid her hands down the side of the baby elephant and gripped it under its front leg.

"I have it!" she said. "I have the leg!" She tried to pull it out, but she was not strong enough. "Help me!" she cried.

Her father wrapped his arms around her waist and pulled. "Don't let go!" he ordered.

She could feel her hands start to slip, but she refused to release her grip. The baby elephant's trunk wrapped even more tightly around her arm. She started to feel the baby elephant's mass give way.

"It's coming!" she yelled, and the mother elephant trumpeted again, forcing the baby out.

Kanita and her father fell backward as the baby elephant plopped out of her mother on top of them covered in birthing goo. The baby struggled, still partially trapped in her amniotic sack. Kanita's father used his kris to cut the sack away.

The baby elephant took her first full gasp of air, and Kanita wrapped her arms around the baby, a baby that was probably ten times the weight of eight-year-old Kanita. A baby girl elephant.

"You did it," her father said, patting her on the back.

Kanita breathed a sigh of relief, happy to have saved the baby elephant and her mother.

But then the mother elephant trumpeted again and let

out a horrifying moan. Blood and other fluids poured out of the mother elephant, soaking the stable floor.

"Oh no!" Kanita cried as she stood, her *chong kraben* drenched with blood. Her feet slipped on the floor as she made her way to the mother elephant's face.

The mother elephant groaned as Kanita stroked her face.

"I'm so sorry," Kanita said. "I'll take care of her. I promise."

The mother elephant sighed one last time, her eyes focusing softly on Kanita as though she understood before closing them forever.

Kanita stood back and then kneeled, kowtowing to the white elephant, thanking her for her service to the king and honoring her as his representative. All of the mahouts in the stables—including Kanita's father—did the same, as was proper. The rest of the elephants in the king's stables—white and gray—let out a mournful trumpet, as though they all suffered from the loss of one of their own.

Kanita was the first to raise her head, as her thoughts were now with the baby elephant left behind. The baby elephant was sitting up, its eyes wide, apparently confused about what was going on. Kanita raised the baby's trunk and coaxed her to follow. She led her to her mother so she could nurse. Even though the mother was dead, the milk she made in preparation for her baby should still be good for the baby's first drink.

As the men discussed what to do next with the deceased royal elephant—they would have to inform the king and then hold a royal procession for her.

Kanita grabbed a bucket of water and started washing the baby. As she did so, she was greeted with an incredible sight.

A Girl and Her Elephant

"Por!" she called to her father. "Look!"

Her father and some of the other mahouts came to see what she was excited about.

"Well, I'll be..." her father trailed off as he sunk to his knees.

The baby—like her mother—was a white elephant.

Once again, everyone in the stables—including Kanita—prostrated themselves before an auspicious elephant.

"Is this the first time a white elephant has been born in captivity?" Kanita asked after they all were standing again.

"King Sakda is truly a blessed monarch," her father said.

"Hey, boss," one of the mahouts said, calling her father to him. He went to him, and the two talked quietly for a moment, frowning at the baby elephant.

"What is it?" Kanita asked. She went to her father's side and realized what they were looking at.

The baby elephant had a long red birthmark down one side of her face. On her pale pink skin—white elephants were not really white, but only a pale gray or pink in color—the mark showed dramatically.

"It's nothing," Kanita said, remembering that her friend Boonsri had a red birthmark on her back. "She's still a white elephant. We will still honor her."

"It's a bad omen elephant, boss," the other mahout mumbled.

"Don't say that!" Kanita yelled.

"Enough," her father said firmly. "I will send an urgent message to the king, telling him what happened and about the new white elephant. In all his wisdom, he will know what to do."

"We should take good care of her," Kanita said. "The king will want to know his auspicious elephant is well cared for."

Kanita went over to the little elephant, who had now finished drinking her mother's milk, and led her to a clean area of the stables. She finished washing and drying the elephant and laid her on a fresh bed of straw.

"Don't worry," Kanita said as she laid down with the elephant, wrapping her arms around her. "I won't let anything happen to you, Safi, my sweet little friend."

But in her heart, she worried about the mahout calling the baby elephant a "bad omen."

From the royal stables in Chiang Mai, it took messages several days to reach the king in Bangkok; and it took many more days for his reply to arrive. During the wait, Kanita busied herself taking care of Safi.

It was a challenge finding the elephant enough milk. There were other young mother elephants in the king's herd, but they were loath to allow Safi to nurse from them too much, lest their own babies not have enough milk to thrive. All day, Kanita would move Safi from one mother elephant to another, hoping the mothers would be kind enough to let Safi nurse. But even then, there was not enough milk to go around. So Kanita spent many hours a day offering to nurse the cows of people in the village in exchange for some of the milk. Kanita stayed with Safi through the night, and Safi would wrap her trunk around Kanita.

After only a few days, Kanita and Safi had bonded in a way that astounded the mahouts, who each had strong bonds with their own elephants.

"Too bad she's a girl," one of the mahouts jokingly said to her father one day. "She has the soul of a mahout."

A Girl and Her Elephant

Kanita's face burned with pride. She hoped that one day her father would defy tradition and let her join the mahouts, but he only shook his head and walked away.

That night, from all the way in the stables, she was awoken by her parents fighting. Kanita tried to slip away from Safi so she could find out what the trouble was, but as soon as she moved, Safi was awake.

"Stay here," Kanita told Safi as she left the stables, but Safi followed closely behind her. "Okay, but at least be quiet!" Kanita warned the elephant.

"This is all your fault," her father yelled at her mother as Kanita snuck to a window and stood on Safi's back to peek in. "You have always spoiled her."

"If that is what you think, you do not know Kanita," her mother said. "She is headstrong and willful. Nothing you or I do will stop her from doing whatever she sets her mind to. She is like a bull elephant. I don't indulge her, I only move out of her way to keep her from trampling over me."

"That is what the ankusha is for," her father snapped, referring to the hook used to control and guide elephants in their training. "You never punish her."

Her mother waved her hands as though to brush off his concerns. "You can criticize my parenting later. The question is, what are we going to do now? You have seen how attached they have grown to each other. This king's edict is going to devastate her."

"There is nothing I can do," he said with a sigh, looking at a piece of paper in his hands stamped with the royal seal. "The elephant must be put to death."

"What?" Kanita shouted, standing up so quickly she lost her balance and fell backward off of Safi.

Her parents ran out of the house and her mother helped

her off the ground, dusting the dirt and leaves from her knees.

"Kanita!" her mother scolded. "What are you doing out so late?"

"He didn't mean it, did he, Mae?" she asked, grasping at her mother. "He's not going to kill Safi!"

Safi let out a worried snuffling sound.

Her mother sighed and held her daughter tight. "I'm sorry, my darling," she said.

"No!" Kanita pulled away from her mother and wrapped her arms around Safi. "You can't! I won't let you!"

"Kanita!" her father said harshly, waving the letter from the king. "The king, in all his wisdom, has deemed the baby elephant a bad omen. She killed her mother. She is marked. She is not a true white elephant, but a cursed one. He has ordered she be put to death lest she bring more sorrow to the elephant herd and the king himself."

"But it's not her fault," Kanita cried. "She's innocent. Just a baby! She needs me!"

"Enough!" Her father snapped as he went back inside the house, leaving Kanita's mother to comfort her daughter.

"I am sorry, my love," she said. "But we cannot defy the king. He knows what is best."

"But he doesn't know Safi!" Kanita cried.

"Shush, child!" her mother cautioned. "You cannot speak against the king!"

Kanita's eyes went wide in horror as her father emerged from their house with his rifle.

"Por! Stop!" Kanita yelled, wrapping her arms more tightly around Safi. "You can't!"

Her father stomped forward, grabbing his daughter roughly by the arm and pulling her away from Safi, who let out a weak, scared trumpeting sound.

A Girl and Her Elephant

"You know how it is, Kanita," her father said, shoving the girl into her mother's arms. "Hold her," he ordered, and her mother held her tightly. He then took a rope and looped it around Safi's neck to lead her away from the house.

"Por! Por! No!" Kanita continued to yell, fighting to escape her mother's grasp.

"Come on, you damn beast," her father grunted as he tried to get Safi to follow him back to the stable, but even though she was a baby, the two-hundred-pound infant was impossible to shift if she didn't want to move, and right now she was too terrified to leave Kanita.

"Fine!" he finally yelled, dropping the rope and aiming his rifle at Safi right there in the yard.

Kanita screamed.

"Hey, boss," one of the mahouts said to get her father's attention.

Kanita and both of her parents looked at the man they hadn't even seen approach. The mahout tossed his head, motioning around the yard. They all looked and realized that the whole village had gathered around to see what the commotion was about. Most of their neighbors were staring, horrified at the scene playing out.

Her father lowered his rifle and shoved the letter from the king at the mahout. "What choice do I have?" he asked.

The mahout read the letter, which he then showed to another mahout who had come over.

Safi had slipped away and back to Kanita's side, who wept as she wrapped her arms around Safi's neck.

The mahouts looked from the letter to Kanita and Safi and then to her father.

"It's just a little elephant, boss," one of the men said, handing the letter back.

"Just a little…" Her father was so stunned at their words

he couldn't finish his sentence. "She'll grow to be just as big as any other elephant. And what about defying the king?"

"I won't tell him if you don't," the mahout said with a goofy grin.

"The gods will know!" her father snapped. "How will they punish me if I defy my king?"

"The gods never punish mercy," Kanita's mother bravely said.

"Why should I show mercy to an elephant?" Kanita's father asked. "Do you have any idea how expensive it will be to raise without the king's blessing?"

"Not mercy for the elephant," her mother hissed. "Mercy for your daughter."

Kanita looked up at her father and begged him with her eyes to do the right thing.

Her father looked at his daughter, his wife, the men in his charge, and the villagers. He let out a frustrated grunt before saying, "Fine! The elephant can live. But I only pray the wrath of the king falls on your heads, not mine."

He stomped back into the house, slamming the door behind him.

It was not until he was out of sight that Kanita was able to stop crying and breathe a sigh of relief.

One of the mahouts went to Kanita's mother's side and patted her back in comfort.

"We are all watching him, Miss Boss," he said, and she nodded her thanks.

"Kanita," her mother said. "Take Safi back to the stables. Everything will be fine."

Kanita was still shaken from the experience and was glad to get back to the safety of the stables.

She took Safi to her stall and laid a blanket over her.

"Don't worry, Safi," Kanita said as they snuggled together and tried to fall asleep. "I'll always protect you. We will always be together. I promise."

CHAPTER TWO

Eight Years Later...

"Whoa! Safi! Look out!" Kanita cried, bouncing along, trying to hold on to Safi's ears as the elephant bounded excitedly toward the river.

Safi trumpeted as she ran into the river for her bath, causing the water to rise suddenly, splashing the other elephants and young mahouts who had been ordered to wash them.

"Kanita!" the boys yelled as they ducked into the water or behind their elephants. "Get out of here!"

Kanita laughed. "What? You think I've never seen a naked boy before? Our mothers used to bathe us together, Chalerm."

"Yeah, then show us your boobs, Kanita!" one of the other boys yelled.

Kanita's face went bright red, and the boys laughed.

"Just wear your *chong kraben* like a normal person so I can swim too," Kanita said. "Safi needs a bath."

At that, Safi filled her trunk with water, which she shot

at Kanita with the power of a cannon, knocking her into the river.

The river was shallow, so Kanita easily found her feet and sputtered as she wiped the water from her face.

"Safi! Shame on you," she said. "Hey, since I'm here, toss me a scrubbing brush, will you?" she called to a boy nearby, but he didn't move to give her the brush. "What's wrong? Got elephant dung in your ears?"

"Come on, Kanita," Chalerm said. "Get out of here. You aren't a real mahout you know."

"But I could be," Kanita said. "I raised an elephant. I trained her. I know more about elephants than any of you. I can be a mahout."

"You know your father wouldn't allow it," Chalerm said. "And girls can't be mahouts anyway. Not *real* mahouts. It's too hard for girls."

"This tattoo on my back says otherwise," Kanita said as she tugged at the back of her shirt enough to show the tattoo between her shoulder blades. All mahouts and their family members were given a sacred tattoo that only mahout families could get. Kanita and her father received the tattoo when they were born. Her mother was given the tattoo on her wedding day.

"That just makes you a mahout's daughter," Chalerm said. "Not a mahout. You're no more a mahout than my old granny!"

Kanita was grateful that her dripping hair hid the tears that were threatening to fall. While she knew their words were true—her father and the other mahouts would never let her join their ranks—they stung coming from her friends. But she knew this moment had been long in coming. Ever since Chalerm first had a crush on her friend Boonsri a couple of years before, she noticed that the division between boys and girls had grown more pronounced. While once all the children played with and bathed the elephants that sustained the village together, one by one, the girls were confined to their homes to learn to cook and clean while the boys spent more time in the jungles, training the elephants and using them to work. Kanita's mother had tried to contain her, to teach her to learn the ways of the home, but Kanita would still spend as much time as she could outside with Safi.

Kanita stuffed her emotions down, deep into her stomach and held her head high. "Fine!" she said. "Let's go, Safi!" Kanita grabbed Safi's ear, and Safi lifted Kanita up with her leg onto her back. "We don't want to play with a bunch of piglets anyway!"

Safi turned out of the river and up the bank, back into the jungle. As soon as they were out of sight of the boys, they could hear them splashing and playing with their elephants once again.

"Kanita!" she heard her mother calling long before they had arrived back in the village. She wondered why her usually docile mother could be yelling for her so frantically.

Safi raised a branch over Kanita's head and the village came into view.

They lived in a small village outside of Chiang Mai, in northern Siam, dedicated to the raising and training of the king's elephants. The king had eleven white elephants, and it was against the law and Heaven to force a white elephant to work, so the white elephants lived in relative peace in the large pastureland and cordoned off area of the jungle just for them. The king also had over fifty elephants that were used to transport the royal family when they traveled, to work on the king's lands, serve in the king's army, and provide whatever other services the king needed. Even though the king lived in Bangkok, the city environment was not the best for elephants, so the king only had ten elephants at his service at any given time in the capital city, and they were rotated regularly so the elephants would have plenty of time in the fresh air of the countryside.

As the king's top mahout, Kanita's father was an important man among the villagers. They had a large teakwood house in the center of the village and lots of land around it for goats and chickens. So, the fact that Kanita's mother's voice was carrying through the village and into the jungle meant that whatever she needed was certainly urgent.

As they exited the jungle and crossed the village toward home, Safi trumpeted to announce their presence.

"Oh! Kanita! Hurry," her mother called, wringing her hands.

Kanita slid down Safi's shoulder and ran to hug her mother. "What is it, Mae?" she asked.

Her mother gripped her wrists to stop the hug. "Look at you! Such a fright. Covered in mud. Stinking of elephant."

"Safi doesn't stink!" Kanita said, stomping her foot.

"Well, you do!" her mother said. "Get inside and wash. Your father has a very important guest coming tonight. Please, you must be on your best behavior."

Kanita groaned but did as she was told. As she entered the house, Safi walked around the outside, from room to room, keeping an eye on her. Safi never let Kanita out of her sight.

"*K*anita," her father called warmly, which she found a little strange since her father was rarely affectionate toward her. "Come, sit by me and meet my new friend, Chakri."

Kanita did as she was told and kneeled on a pillow on the floor at her father's side. She glanced to the window and smiled at Safi, who was peeking in at them. "I am happy to meet you, Naai Chankri," she said politely.

Chakri smiled and nodded to Kanita's father. "Very polite," he said approvingly. "You have trained her well."

Chakri was considerably older than Kanita, at least in his forties, and he was dark skinned from the sun and already wrinkled. But Kanita could tell from his clothes and gold bangles that he must be wealthy, and for some reason her father wanted to impress this man, so she kept her head bowed and her mouth closed.

"You are too kind," her father said. "I'm sure you are aware of my daughter's wild reputation."

Chakri laughed. "Nothing a good husband with a firm hand won't easily correct."

Kanita's head shot up at the mention of the word husband. She looking worryingly at her mother, who was sitting silently across the room, not meeting her gaze.

"In truth, it was that wild nature that first drew my attention," Chakri told Kanita's father. "Many years ago, my wife died in childbirth. The child died as well. I was greatly distraught. I wandered, mindless, into the jungle. I happened upon a beautiful girl in a river, playing with her baby elephant. The sun was shining and the water sparkled. It was as though Heaven was telling me that there was still hope in the world."

A Girl and Her Elephant

Kanita's father put a hand to her shoulder and squeezed. She looked up at him and saw him beaming with pride. It was the first time her father had ever looked at her like that. She was so conflicted. She was glad to have brought Chakri comfort in his hour of despair, but the fact he had been watching her in the river years ago—when she still would have been a child—made her skin crawl. She tried once again to catch her mother's eye and noticed that her mother was glaring at Chakri, something neither Chakri nor her father seemed to notice. At the window, Safi snuffled loudly.

"I have thought of that girl many times over the years," Chakri continued. "But only recently did I hear about the girl and her elephant, the daughter of the king's mahout. So, I came here in search of her and was so glad to find the same little girl again. And when I learned that she was still available for marriage, well, could anything else be so destined by the stars?"

"Wait," Kanita finally said, and her father gripped her shoulder tighter. "What is happening?"

"Kanita," her father said. "Chakri has asked for your hand in marriage, and he has offered a generous bride price."

Kanita twisted her shoulder from her father's grip and stood up. "But I don't want to be married," she said. "I want to help you with the elephants."

"Stop this nonsense," her father said, doing his best to keep his temper in check. "You are a girl, not a mahout. Your only path in life is to marry."

Kanita feared this day would come, but never imagined it would be so soon. She had been living in denial since it was common for girls her age to be married.

"But I am not ready," Kanita said. "I cannot keep house.

I cannot cook."

"Chakri is already aware of how your mother has failed you," her father said. Kanita looked to her mother pleadingly, but she still had her eyes averted, her hands to her mouth as though to stave off tears. "But he has agreed to marry you anyway."

"My mother is more than willing to oversee your training," Chakri interjected.

"A more generous or kind offer is not likely to come our way, Kanita," her father said. "I have already accepted Chakri's proposal."

"Por!" she said to her father dropping to her knees again and clasping her hands in front of her. "Please, reconsider. I'll be a better daughter, I promise! Please don't send me and Safi away!"

"Who is Safi?" Chakri asked.

"Her elephant," her father grumbled.

Chakri nodded. "Ah, yes. The bad omen elephant."

"Don't call her that!" Kanita said.

"Kanita!" Her father gripped her arm and shook her. "You will speak with respect to your betrothed."

She felt the bile rise in her throat at her father calling Chakri her betrothed.

"Your father and I have already discussed the elephant, sweet Kanita," Chakri said, laying a hand on her father's shoulder to calm him. "Your father showed you great mercy and kindness in allowing the elephant to live. You should honor him all your days for that. But no, you cannot bring the elephant to live with us. The elephant is bad luck. I cannot have it near my home."

"I cannot leave Safi," Kanita said, suddenly more terrified of being separated from Safi than of having to marry Chakri. "We have bonded, just like any mahout and elephant. She thinks I'm her mother, her family. She can't live without me."

"Then maybe the kind thing would be to put the elephant down," Chakri said. "Better than have her die of a broken heart or starve to death."

"Don't say that!" Kanita said, pulling away from her father's hand and stepping away. "I can't leave Safi! I promised that I would never leave her."

At the window, Safi shuffled back and forth, letting out an irritated groan. She could tell that Kanita was in distress and was responding in kind.

"Sweet Kanita," Chakri said, standing. "Your devotion to your elephant is admirable. It shows what a caring and attentive mother you will be when you have your own children."

Kanita did not hide her feelings of revulsion at this thought. "I will never have children with you," she said without thinking.

At that, her father stepped forward and slapped her across the face.

Safi trumpeted loudly, and Kanita gasped in shock and pain.

Her mother jumped to her feet. "Kasem!" she said softly, the first word she had uttered all evening.

Kanita looked at her father, tears burning her eyes.

"The elephant is bad luck," her father said. Kanita wanted to protest, but the rage was still present in his eyes, so she said nothing. "Had I known that the elephant would render you unmarriageable, I would have killed her as I was ordered to do. Heaven is punishing me for defying my king!"

Kanita sank to her knees and did not stop the tears from flowing. "Por! I beg you! Please spare Safi! I'll do anything! Please, don't kill my elephant!"

Her father and Chakri whispered among themselves for a moment.

"If you agree to marry Chakri," her father said, "I will only release the elephant into the wild. I won't kill her."

This was still not good enough for Kanita. Anything short of keeping Safi with her for the rest of her life was not something she could accept. But if she agreed, it would at least buy her time to come up with a plan for them to be together.

"I will only agree," Kanita finally said, "if I am the one to turn Safi out."

"It is agreed," Chakri said.

CHAPTER THREE

Kanita walked outside, and Safi was waiting for her by the door. Winding her trunk around Kanita's hand, the two walked to the stables. They walked past the stall where Safi's mother had died many years before, a red stain on the floor that had never quite faded away, a haunting reminder of the tragedy that forever linked Kanita and Safi together.

When they reached Safi's stall—one she didn't really use since she typically slept outside Kanita's bedroom window—Kanita picked up an old horsehair brush and ran it over Safi's large stomach. Safi laid down and lolled to one side so Kanita could rub the brush along her backbone.

"That man..." Kanita whispered, looking around to make sure no one could hear her. "I don't trust him. I don't think he will be a good husband."

Safi let out a sigh, blowing dust and hay across the floor.

"You think so too?" Kanita asked. "He's just so...weird! What was he talking about? Seeing me as just a little girl? Gross! I'm sorry he lost his wife, but why did he then turn his attention to me? I can't replace her. I can't be a good wife like her. Por was right about that, I have not learned how to cook or clean house like I should have."

Safi grunted and waved her trunk at Kanita.

"I don't regret it!" Kanita said with a laugh. "I was never happier than when I was riding you through the forest. But...but what am I supposed to do now?"

Her motions slowed as she ran her fingers over the short, sharp elephant hairs of Safi's back. She picked at the hard, pale skin.

"Por...he wants me to marry that dreadful man and..." Her voice dropped to barely a whisper. "And turn you out..."

Safi rolled to a sitting position and let out a loud trumpet.

"Shh!" Kanita said, waving her hands to get Safi's attention. "Quiet! Don't make Por angry."

Safi let out a groan as she lowered her trunk. She wrapped her trunk around Kanita and pulled her in for a hug.

Kanita laid her head against the elephant's broad face.

"I promised your mother I would take care of you," she said. "I will keep my promise."

"Are you talking to that elephant?"

Kanita gasped and turned to face her mother.

"Don't act surprised," Kanita said. "I tell Safi everything."

Her mother chuckled. "I am certain of that," she said as she took another brush from a nearby shelf and moved to brush one of Safi's large legs.

The two women brushed Safi in silence for a moment. Kanita knew her mother had been sent by her father to make sure she turned Safi out. It was just one more way her father continued to treat them cruelly, turning them against each other. Kanita did not want to fight, she knew her father would punish her mother if she failed to get Kanita to do as he wished. But she couldn't turn out Safi! She wasn't sure what to do, so they just brushed Safi in silence.

"By the time I was your age," her mother finally said, "I had been married six months."

"I know," Kanita said.

"Your father, he hasn't changed in the slightest from our wedding day," her mother continued. "Just as hard-headed. Just as exacting." She sighed. "It's exhausting trying to live up to his standards."

Kanita nodded, but still didn't look at her mother.

"The one bright spot in my life has been you," she said.

Kanita felt tears well in her eyes, but she didn't want to cry. She knew she was going to let her parents down by refusing to release Safi. She didn't care about disappointing her father, but her mother...She hated to cause her grief.

Her mother gripped her shoulders and forced her to face her.

"My darling," she said. "I know you are scared, and angry. But you knew that one day you would have to marry. No amount of refusing to cook and clean was going to prevent a marriage forever."

"I know," Kanita mumbled.

"Then what are you so afraid of?" her mother asked. "It is just the nature of things. A woman will leave her parents and go to the home of her husband."

"I don't care about that," Kanita snapped, pulling away, shocked that her mother couldn't see the real reason why she was upset. "I care about Safi! She's the only thing in the world that matters to me."

"The only thing?" her mother asked, crossing her arms.

Kanita sighed. "And you, Mae. But, as you say, I knew I would have to leave you. I never thought I would have to leave Safi. I thought I could bring her with me. That any man who wanted me would also accept Safi."

"Elephants are expensive, my love," her mother said. "You were only able to keep Safi because we have to feed so many other elephants anyway."

"I know," Kanita sighed. "Maybe I was foolish to think I would marry a man rich enough to afford an elephant, but...but what am I supposed to do? Mae, Safi loves me. I'm the only mother she knows. If I turn her out, if I abandon her, she will die. I am certain of it."

"Oh," her mother cried, pulling Kanita into her chest. "I know Safi is only eight years old, but for an elephant, she is an adult. She will be fine."

"No, Mae," Kanita said. "She doesn't know how to find water. She doesn't wash herself. She doesn't associate with the other elephants. It's like they think she's...odd."

"Maybe she is," her mother said. "The other elephants, they bond to their mahout and each other. I agree that Safi is too close to you. But I am sure she will not die. Let me talk to Por. Maybe we can keep Safi here instead of turning her out."

"I don't trust Por," Kanita said. "He has always believed that Safi is a bad luck elephant. I think...I think that if I leave her behind, he will kill her."

Safi sat up and trumpeted again. Kanita and her mother jumped back as Safi started to pace, swinging her trunk in distress at the tone in Kanita's voice.

"Safi! Safi!" Kanita said, holding up her hands. "Calm! Calm! I'm here. You don't need to worry."

Safi slowed her pacing and then stopped next to Kanita, who hugged Safi's leg and petted her softly.

"See, Mae," Kanita said. "Safi needs me."

Her mother had been standing there in shock, her

hands to her mouth. It was as though she hadn't realized the strength of the bond between the elephant and her daughter until that moment. She turned away and paced for a moment.

"Kanita," she finally said. "I...I have something for you." She reached into her pocket and pulled out a velvet bag, which she placed into Kanita's hand. "It is from Chakri. Your *khong man*, part of your dower gift."

Kanita opened the bag and gasped when she saw a dozen solid gold bracelets. Chakri was a wealthy man indeed. Kanita was surprised her mother gave her the *khong man*. Usually, the parents would keep it until the bride wore it on her wedding day.

Kanita looked up at her mother knowing she only had questions painted on her face.

"I know that you will do the right thing," her mother said. She then leaned in, kissed Kanita on her forehead, and left the stables.

It was now Kanita's turn to pace. What did her mother mean by that? What was the right thing to do with so much gold? What did it have to do with Safi? She peeked out of the stables at the house and saw her father waiting impatiently on the porch. She could not hear him, but she could tell he was berating her mother as she approached him. Anger welled up in her belly. She hated the way her father treated her mother. And she hated the way he treated her. She wouldn't stand for it any longer. She wouldn't live a life of captivity and misery with Chakri.

As if reading her mind, when she turned back, Safi was already in a kneeling position, waiting for Kanita to climb onto her back. Kanita ran to her, gripped her ear, and flung herself behind Safi's enormous head in one fluid leap.

"Let's get out of here!" Kanita said. She had no idea

where they would go or what they would do, but they would have each other.

And Chakri's bag of gold.

Safi trumpeted as she flung the doors to the stable open and galloped into the yard. Kanita's father saw them and ran after them, yelling for them to come back.

"Get back here right now!" he ordered.

Kanita stared to raise her arm in a goodbye wave, but then she saw Chakri come outside behind him and thought better of it. Something about that man unnerved her. She hoped she would never have to see him again, though she realized he would not be happy about her taking the bag of *khong man* and not getting a bride in return.

Oh well, Kanita thought. *He can afford it.*

"Come on," Kanita said, tapping Safi on the head by her right ear. "Out the back gate. Into the jungle!"

Safi let out an excited grunt as she turned toward the back of the grazing pasture. They ran past some of the other elephants whose mahouts had not yet put them away for the night. Safi trumpeted at them, as if to tell them that she was leaving on an adventure, and they began to trumpet and run around in excitement as well.

Kanita laughed as she felt the cool wind on her face and Safi's great girth lumbering up and down beneath her. She had to hold on tight to keep from being tossed off.

At the growing noise of the elephants and Kanita's screaming parents, other villagers and mahouts came out of their homes to see what the ruckus was. As they saw the large group of elephants heading for the back gate, they too began to yell at Kanita and Safi and the other elephants as they ran along the fencing.

Kanita saw many of the village children squealing with

delight as she passed them, which only gave her more encouragement.

Some of the elephants broke off from the group at the urging of their mahouts, but most of them kept running, gaining speed. The gate came into view, and Kanita could feel Safi slow in hesitation under her.

"Come on, girl!" Kanita urged. "Don't stop now! We are going to be free!"

Safi trumpeted and picked up speed as she headed for the gate. Kanita crouched down as they approached, using Safi's large ears to protect herself.

The gate was solid wood, but not very thick. It was never designed to stop an elephant stampede. While it was always known that the elephants could break the gate—or any part of the fence—if they really tried, none of the elephants had ever wanted to. The fencing around the elephant pasture was more of a guide to keep the elephants and humans separated.

Still, Safi and the other elephants crashed through the gate with their full might, sending shards of wood flying in every direction. Once they were out, Kanita rose up high on Safi's back and waved back at the village. The other elephants slowed, one by one, not really feeling the urge to leave their home, but Safi and Kanita rode onward, to the end of the road, and into the thick overgrown jungle beyond.

Kanita could still hear the yells—and some laughs—from the village behind her. Her parents would be furious, and probably never forgive her. The other elephants would have to be rounded up and the gate repaired. The other families would want to know, "What's gotten into Kanita?" Her father would have to explain why his daughter had acted so recklessly. What would he say? That she was a fool for running from a good marriage? That she had always been a rebellious child? Probably.

Would he let her mother take the blame?

Her nostrils flared at the thought and she squeezed the bag of gold in her pocket. She hoped that this was what her mother had meant by telling her to do the right thing.

What could be more right than fighting for your freedom?

CHAPTER FOUR

"Did you hear that?" Kanita asked Safi as her eyes darted from left to right, but Safi only let out a snuffle. Kanita was sure she had heard the snap of a twig, like someone walking through the brush nearby. But in the dark, even by the light of the half-moon, she saw nothing.

Safi had run for nearly an hour, crashing through the thick growth of the forest while Kanita hugged the elephant's sides with her legs, her hands gripped tight to Safi's ears. She had kept her head down to keep from being knocked off by low branches. They were well away from the village now, but Kanita had no idea where they actually were. She had not had much reason to leave the village, and she never went beyond the fences at night. Nothing here looked familiar. Everywhere she looked there were only bushes, trees, and vines.

The sounds of the jungle at night were not a comfort either. Clicking, skittering, and groaning noises surrounded her, assaulting her ears. Her stomach rumbled, and as the excitement of their dramatic escape from the village wore off, her eyelids began to droop.

As they lumbered along, Safi grabbed random leaves and brush and stuffed them into her mouth.

"Must be nice to be able to eat anything that crosses our path," Kanita said.

Safi lifted her trunk to Kanita holding a leaf the size of Kanita's head in it.

Kanita pushed the trunk away. "I'm not that desperate yet," she said. "Though I might be by morning."

Safi grunted and shoved the leaf in her mouth.

Kanita shivered and rubbed her arms with her hands. It wasn't really cold, but the dampness of the cool night air settled on her skin, making her miss the woven blanket back on her own bed.

Kanita hmphed to herself. She hadn't even been gone two hours and was already missing home? *Better get used to it*, she thought. She couldn't go back, not ever. If she went back, willingly or by force, she'd have to marry that awful Chakri! Such a weird and gross old man. She couldn't imagine having to be his wife. And when he mentioned children, she thought she was going to be sick on the floor right there!

Not to mention that she'd be separated from Safi.

Safi!

When they ran away together, Kanita had only thought of them staying together. She hadn't considered what would happen to Safi if they were caught.

She'd probably be put to death.

Many of the villagers, not to mention her own father, had worried about Safi being a bad luck elephant. Everyone who knew Safi knew that Kanita's family had defied the king by not killing her as a baby. But the villagers were like a big family. None of them would ever betray Kanita's father by telling the king that the bad luck elephant still lived.

A Girl and Her Elephant

Until now.

Now that Kanita and Safi had left the village—and left destruction in their wake—would the other villagers alert the king about what her father had done? He would be ruined. Her father was the king's highest-ranking mahout. He, as his father and grandfather had done, trained all of the king's elephants, not just the white ones.

The white elephants did not work. They were a gift from heaven, so their lives were ones of pleasure and leisure. To harm a white elephant was worthy of death.

Unless that elephant was cursed.

Kanita couldn't recall another time in history when a white elephant had also been a cursed elephant. In fact, she couldn't remember hearing about more than two or three cursed elephants in her life. Elephants were highly regarded, honored among all the people. The elephants were not only revered, but were a necessary part of life. Elephants provided much of the labor they needed to build their homes and clear their fields. Without elephants, the Siamese way of life could not exist. To order the death of an elephant, any elephant, was a grave undertaking, never considered lightly and usually avoided at all costs. The only other elephants Kanita could remember who had received such a sentence were bull elephants who had gone rogue and killed their masters. Safi hadn't killed anyone, but by charging out of the village like that, the villagers probably saw killing her as an act of self-preservation.

Not to mention the fact that the king had already ordered it years ago! Safi and Kanita running away, destroying the fencing, and riling up the other elephants could be seen by some as a punishment for defying the king.

The villagers probably saw two options. They could find

Safi and kill her, thus ending the bad luck brought by the elephant and by disobeying the king. Or they could report Kanita's father to the king so the king could exact divine justice upon him, thus also freeing the village from the elephant's curse.

Kanita felt nauseous. What had she done? She had doomed her family and the elephant she had only meant to save. But if she went back, if she were able to save her father, Safi would still be killed.

Kanita couldn't see a way out of the mess she had made. Tears began rolling down her cheeks.

Safi raised her trunk to Kanita's face and let out a little cry of her own.

"Oh, don't worry about me," Kanita said. "I've just done something very stupid and I'm not sure how to get us out of it."

Kanita's stomach growled again. She hadn't eaten dinner, her stomach in too much turmoil since her father had shared his terrible decision to marry her to Chakri before they had even sat down to eat. Safi let out a worried moan.

"I'm fine," Kanita said. "This won't be the first night I've been punished with no dinner. But tomorrow..." She would have to find food eventually. Hopefully, by the light of day, they would be able to find bananas and coconuts, but she wouldn't be able to live on what she could forage forever. Eventually, she would need more substantial sustenance.

As Safi slowly plodded down a small hill, the gold bangles in her pouch jingled. If they came across a village, she could trade the bangles for cash and use that to buy food.

But then she realized that Safi would follow her wherever she went. If they went into a village—any village—

A Girl and Her Elephant

word of their location would eventually get back to her father. He would find her.

"We have to get out of here," Kanita said. Safi grunted. "No, not just out of the jungle, but out of Siam," Kanita continued. "You aren't safe here. We aren't safe. If I am caught, I'll be forced to marry Chakri. If you are caught...I... I can't think about it."

Something flapped its wings wildly near Kanita's head. She gasped and ducked. Safi trumpeted and picked up her pace again, bouncing Kanita along.

"Whoa! Whoa! Slow down!" Kanita cried, gripping Safi's ears. "It was just a bat!"

Safi came to a quick stop, causing Kanita to fall forward over Safi's face. Thankfully, her firm grip with her thighs kept her from completely falling off.

Kanita grunted as she climbed back up to her spot behind Safi's head. She rubbed her back and her neck as she stretched.

"I think we must both be getting tired," Kanita said, but she knew she was probably the only one who was really tired. Safi only needed about two hours of sleep a night, and she got it while standing up. She would only lay down for a longer sleep every few days, and she had just had that kind of sleep the night before.

"Just walk slow, okay?" Kanita said, and Safi let out a little sniff. Kanita rolled over onto her back and looked up at the stars while Safi ambled along. "I just wish I knew where we were going. I think we need to leave Siam. We have to get you out of here. Everywhere we go, every village we try to enter, the people will recognize you."

Kanita felt her eyes get heavier as Safi's swaying gait rocked her to sleep. She let her legs dangle over each side to help keep her from rolling too far one way or another.

"I know that China's not far," Kanita said. "We can travel north, through Burma, and be in China in only a couple of days. Then we'd be free."

Safi let out a low moan.

"I don't speak Burmese or Chinese," Kanita said. "But I can learn. There must be many people on the border who speak many languages, don't you think? I'm sure it must be necessary for trade. Maybe I can use the gold to hire someone to teach me Chinese. China is a huge country. Millions of *rai* big. We could get lost in China and no one would ever find us."

Yes, going to China seemed to be the best way to keep Safi safe. The Chinese didn't revere elephants the way the Siamese did, but they wouldn't have such superstitions about them either, Kanita reasoned. They wouldn't see a white elephant with a pink birthmark as a bad omen elephant, but just as an elephant.

But that wouldn't save her father from whatever punishment the king might decide to mete out if he learned of his betrayal.

Pain gnawed at Kanita's stomach, this time from guilt. But what could she do? She could either save her father or her elephant.

And her elephant was winning that battle.

She couldn't believe her father wanted to just hand her over to Chakri without considering her. Of course, she knew it was up to parents to make marriage arrangements for their children, and eventually she would have to marry whoever her father chose. But many parents at least took their children's feelings into account. If a young woman were firm in her refusal, most parents would reject a proposed match. Kanita wasn't ready to marry. And she certainly did not want to marry a creepy old man. A man who refused to accept Safi.

If only her father had waited and chosen someone else. Someone younger. Someone who would understand that Safi was a part of Kanita's life.

What was it her father had said? "A better offer is not likely to come our way," or something like that. She was only sixteen! And this was the first offer of marriage she had received. Surely she had many years of marriage proposals ahead of her. It was as though her father had already given up on her.

Fine. If her father had given up on her, then she had already given up on him. She and Safi would go to China and live a long happy life together. Chakri's gold would get them by until they found a place to live and Kanita either found work or a nice *young* husband who also loved elephants.

Everything would be perfect.

As she drifted off to sleep, she refused to think about her mother and the hell her father was probably putting her through right now for raising such a useless, rebellious child.

CHAPTER FIVE

Kanita awoke to the sound of rushing water. She opened her eyes and felt the sun's warming rays on her skin. Birds tweeted their morning song as they fluttered overhead.

Kanita sat up and realized that Safi was standing at the edge of a wide river and was using her trunk to take large refreshing gulps. She tapped Safi's head, giving her the signal to lean down on one side so she could jump down. She walked to the river's edge and stepped into the cool water. She cupped the water with her hands and washed her face and arms. She then took a long drink herself.

"Where are we?" Kanita asked, but Safi just kept drinking her water. She sighed. She remembered wanting to head to China, but she had no idea where they were or which direction they should be going. Was there a river like this on the way to China? She tried to recall a map she had seen, showing Siam, Burma, and China, but she couldn't remember the details. She knew Laos was also to the north and east, but she wasn't sure how safe it was. Laos was occupied by French colonizers who didn't get along with the

A Girl and Her Elephant

British leaders who were currently in Siam. She didn't know a lot about the politics of the foreigners, but she thought it best to steer as clear away from them as possible.

Once again, her stomach rumbled, loudly this time. She needed to find food. She looked around but didn't see any fruit trees. She patted Safi on the leg, and she kneeled down so Kanita could climb back up on her. They walked along the river, Kanita unsure if they should cross it or not. She had no idea which way they should be going, but she was afraid to seek out any villages or villagers to ask for directions. She couldn't risk anyone seeing Safi and reporting back to her father.

A familiar pungent scent wafted past her nose and her mouth watered. Up ahead, she saw a grove of durian trees.

"Back, back! Into the woods," Kanita ordered Safi, who did as she was told.

Kanita's mouth watered at the thought of grabbing one of the durians and digging into its delicious flesh, but she couldn't let her hunger overrun her brain. They had to be cautious. If there was a durian grove, then there could be farmers nearby tending and guarding the trees.

Kanita slapped at her neck and then her arm as mosquitoes in the shade took bites of her. She waited a few minutes, and when no farmers appeared, she urged Safi to move toward the durian grove slowly and quietly. Once they were close enough, Safi reached up with her trunk and pulled one of the durians free. Then Kanita urged Safi back into the jungle.

Kanita jumped down, ready to dig into the delicious fruit when she realized she had a problem.

"I don't have a knife," she said as she surveyed the durian's tough, thorn-covered skin. There was no way she was going to be able to get into the fruit herself without ruining her hands in the process. "Okay, Safi," Kanita said as she motioned for Safi to raise her foot and she placed the durian under it. "Just lower your foot nice and easy and crack the shell, okay? Lower it easy...easy."

Safi put her foot down, crushing the durian flat into the mud.

Kanita looked back toward the grove, still not seeing or hearing any farmers.

"It's okay," Kanita said. "We will just get another one and try again."

This time, Kanita did not bother climbing back up on Safi. She took Safi by the trunk, and they crept back toward the durian grove. Safi yanked a durian from the tree, and they slunk back into the jungle.

"Okay," Kanita said as she placed the durian under Safi's foot. "Let's try again. But be gentle. Go slowly...slowly."

Safi crushed the durian with her foot, grinding it into the earth.

Kanita, her stomach eating at her with starvation as the strong smell of the durian infiltrated her nose, put her face in her hands to stifle a scream.

"Okay, okay," Kanita said, calming herself. "This isn't working. You can't do it. I need to think about your training and what you *can* do." She led Safi back to the durian grove to steal another one while she tried to come up with a plan.

"I think I've got it," Kanita said, placing the durian under Safi's foot. "This time, you are going to put your foot down, and then up very quickly. Understand?"

Safi snuffled.

"Down," Kanita said, watching the durian anxiously. "Down...down...Up!"

She said up just as Safi's foot came down on the durian, but with her lumbering, slow moving form, she wasn't able

A Girl and Her Elephant

to then pull back up in time and once again crushed the durian with her foot.

Kanita fell backward onto the ground. "Safi!" she cried.

Safi picked up some of the crushed bit of durian in her snout, along with some of the dirt it had been smashed into, and offered it to Kanita.

"Eww," Kanita said, pushing the snotty mass away. "It's okay. We can try one more time. I just need to have you lift your foot sooner. Come on."

Together they stole another durian, and Kanita positioned it under Safi's foot once again.

"One more time," Safi said. "We can do this. Down...Up!"

Kanita's heart froze in her chest as she heard a cracking sound. But when she moved Safi's raised foot out of the way she saw that the durian was still mostly intact!

"You did it!" Kanita said as she gleefully pulled the shell of the durian apart, revealing the yellow fruit inside. She pried some of the fruit free and sighed as she put it in her mouth. "Good job, Safi," she said, exhausted from the effort but relieved to finally have some food in her belly.

"Hey! What's that?" she heard a man yell.

Kanita grabbed the durian and patted Safi's leg. "We better go!" she said as she climbed up.

She heard footsteps and more yelling as farmers ran in their direction. "Get out of here, you damn beast!" one of them yelled. Then she heard one of them cock a rifle.

"Run!" Kanita yelled. Safi let out a trumpet as she bounded through the forest when they heard the crack of a rifle fired in their direction. Kanita let out a scream and ducked her head. As her hands flew up to protect her ears, she dropped her durian.

They ran deep into the jungle, away from the river and

the durian grove. Kanita's neck and arm itched where the mosquitoes had bitten her, but she didn't dare let go as Safi continued to run. The shot from the rifle had scared Safi so badly, Kanita was sure she wouldn't stop running until she got tired, which for an elephant could take a while.

She had no idea how far Safi had run. They were no longer in the jungle but were running across an open plain. It was nearing mid-day, and the sun was beating down on Kanita. She was sweating profusely and she could feel the skin on her back burning.

"Safi!" she said, patting the elephant on the back on her head. "You can stop now. We are okay!"

But Safi continued bounding along. In and out of the jungle. Up and down hills. Cashing through the brush and trampling small trees.

Kanita bounced on top of the elephant's back. Her body stiff and sore from hanging on so long and not getting enough sleep. Sweating and stinking. Every part of her itching.

"Safi! Stop!" Kanita finally screamed, at her wit's end.

Safi let out a trumpet that ricocheted through the jungle and came to a sudden halt, sending Kanita over Safi's face and flat on her back on the ground. The wind was completely knocked out of her as dust circled. She coughed, trying to catch a breath.

"Safi," Kanita moaned as she rolled to her side. "What's gotten into you?"

But before Safi could indicate a reply, Kanita gasped. The sand around her started to move and she began to sink. Safi grunted and moved backward as her feet started to sink too.

Kanita tried to scramble to her feet as the ground started to give way beneath her.

"Safi!" she screamed, holding out her hand as she sunk into the quicksand. "Help me!"

From the edge of the sand pit, Safi reached for Kanita's hand with her trunk. She wrapped her trunk around Kanita's arm and pulled. Kanita kicked her legs free and breathed a sigh of relief when she reached the firm ground safely.

"Thanks, Safi," she said, patting the elephant's leg.

For a moment, exhaustion seemed to overtake them both, so they sat in silence and listened to the sounds of the forest. The clicking. The skittering. The groaning.

"If we aren't careful, Safi," Kanita said, "we are going to die out here." She sighed and wiped her mouth with the back of her hand, which ended up only getting more sand and dirt in her mouth. She was filthy and felt worse. "Come on," she said, standing and climbing on Safi's back. "Let's make our way back to the river so I can clean up."

Safi snorted as she rose up, carrying Kanita in a new direction, one they hadn't come from nor had been going in. Kanita had no idea if they were traveling toward the river or not. She just needed to rest.

Safi carried Kanita at a slow, easy pace so as not to jostle her too much. Kanita refused to cry even though she couldn't imagine feeling lower than she did right now. They were completely lost. Safi didn't have many needs, other than her need to be with Kanita. But Kanita faced more urgent issues. She had no food. She didn't have clothes to change into. She had nowhere safe to sleep. And there was no one she could ask for help.

But she couldn't go back home. She couldn't give up. She had promised to take care of Safi, and she would see that promise through. Somehow, they would find a way to survive together.

They finally came to a small river. It wasn't the wide rushing one they had been at that morning, but it would do. Kanita dropped from Safi's back and waded into the water. She washed her face, her arms, her torso. She drank in the thirst-quenching water. Then she untied her hair and soaked it in the water. Safi wandered into the river as well, laying on her side and spraying herself with the water.

After a few minutes, Kanita started to feel better. Cleaner, certainly. But also refreshed. Rejuvenated. She walked over and ran her hands over Safi's side to get some of the clots of mud off of her. She didn't even have a brush with her to wash her clean. She should have planned her escape a little better. Brought some bare necessities with her if nothing else. If they came across a village, maybe she could somehow convince Safi to stay in the jungle just long enough to do a little bit of trading.

She was going over a list of the things she would buy if given the chance when she heard voices. Her pulse raced as she moved toward the river's edge, but then she saw that it was only a group of children who had come to the river to play at the end of a hot day. They were far enough away, she couldn't get a good look at them, so she figured they couldn't see her very clearly either. A girl in the river with her elephant wouldn't be anything unusual. As long as they weren't close enough to see Safi's birthmark, Safi and Kanita should be safe from a bunch of kids. Still, she couldn't help but feel a little nervous.

"Come on, Safi," she said at last. "We should get going. We need to find me more food."

Safi sat up and let the water rush off of her enormous body.

Then they both heard a scream.

"Help!" a young boy called out. "I'm caught!"

A Girl and Her Elephant

Kanita watched as a young boy's head bobbed up and down in the water, his mouth gasping for air. He must have been snagged by a branch or caught in the current. The other children started to panic. Some ran around on the shore. Others started to swim out toward their friend, but then got scared and swam away. A few ran into the jungle, probably to go find their parents for help.

Safi started to cross the river toward the boy, but Kanita held her back.

"No, Safi!" Kanita ordered. "We can't let them see us. It's not our problem. Come on." She patted Safi's leg, but Safi did not raise it up. She shuffled her feet back and forth and made whimpering sounds.

"We can't!" Kanita said, even though it would be so easy for Safi to help the boy. Even if the water was deep, Safi could swim over, grab the boy with her trunk, and take him safely to the river's edge.

But everyone would remember the marked white elephant who saved the boy's life.

They would be caught for sure.

"Come on," Kanita growled, slapping Safi's leg harder. Safi finally, reluctantly, raised her leg and lifted Kanita to her back.

"He's drowning!" one of the girls screamed.

Kanita looked back at the boy and saw that his head was still bobbing up and down, but he was no longer gasping for air. Her heart stung. Only a few minutes before, Safi had saved her life. Now, she was denying another child that same chance.

Was this the person her mother wanted her to be?

"My boy!" a woman screamed. Kanita looked toward the shore and saw a woman and several men run out of the jungle. The woman held her hands to her face as the men charged into the river. She must have been the boy's mother.

"Come on," Kanita whispered, kicking Safi's side with her heel. "Let's get out of here."

With the arrival of the adults, there was nothing more that Safi or Kanita could do to help. Yet, Kanita could not help but look back and watch as the men worked to free the boy from whatever was holding him down. Finally, they were able to drag his limp body from the water and toward the shore to his frantic mother. The people all went back into the jungle, most likely back to their village and local healer to try and save him.

She couldn't tell if the boy was alive or dead. She prayed he was alive, but her heart hurt over the real possibility that he had drowned.

And it was her fault.

She should have let Safi help. But she was scared. If Safi had been recognized. If her father found them. Safi might have saved that boy's life, but then she would have lost her own. She had to protect Safi.

No matter the cost.

CHAPTER SIX

Safi reached up and plucked a bunch of bananas from a tree and handed them to Kanita.

"Oh, finally!" Kanita said as she peeled open a banana and ate it in nearly one gulp. Then she ate another one, and another. Safi let out a grunt. "Okay, okay, I'll slow down," Kanita said with a sigh as she sat down and leaned up against a tree, savoring the sweet taste of the banana. But as the food settled in her stomach, she started to feel a little queasy. Between the bananas and durian, she'd only had sweet fruits to eat for days, which seemed to be irritating her stomach. She would need to find something else to eat soon, some vegetables or beans, maybe some meat. But she was still too scared to try and approach any villages.

The sun was setting, and Kanita was feeling sore and exhausted.

"We need to find a place for me to sleep," Kanita said to Safi. "It's too hard on my body to sleep on your back. I need to lay flat. But we can't be exposed."

Even though she was tired, Kanita walked, leading Safi through the jungle, away from the river. She needed the exercise to keep her mind off that poor boy. She knew that she had done the right thing in terms of protecting Safi, but she couldn't escape the guilt gnawing at her heart.

They finally came across a jagged rockface. As they started to move around it, they found a small indentation. It wasn't exactly a cave, but it was deep enough that Kanita wouldn't feel exposed from all sides. And she knew Safi would watch over her as she slept.

The ground of the cave was only dirt and rocks, so she and Safi worked together to gather enough palm fronds to make Kanita a small bed. Then Kanita gathered a bunch of fern leaves to make a pillow. She covered herself with more palm fronds to keep the bugs and cool night air away from her skin. She finally collapsed in the bed, looking up at the cave ceiling as she waited to fall asleep.

"Everything will be fine," Kanita said as Safi stood nearby. "We just have to look out for ourselves. You and me, Safi. You and me forever…"

The snap of a twig woke Kanita from her sleep and she sat up straight. She felt her body break out in gooseflesh as she tried to survey her surroundings in the dark. But she didn't hear anything else out of the ordinary. She heard the usual creaking, squeaking, groaning, but she should have gotten used to the sounds of the jungle by now.

But something felt different.

"Safi?" she called out softly, and she heard Safi shuffle her feet in response.

She sighed in relief. It was probably just Safi who stepped on a branch, making the noise. She laid back down and tried to will herself to go back to sleep, but she felt

A Girl and Her Elephant

agitated now, unable to relax. She got up and wandered out of the cave. There was a slight breeze blowing, so she rubbed her arms, wishing she had one of her mother's woven wraps with her.

Outside the cave, the moon was brighter than the previous night, and she could make out some of the trees nearby. Safi wandered away from the cave and stripped some leaves off of a tree and put them in her mouth.

Kanita turned to go back into the cave and then screamed.

"Gotcha!" Chakri yelled as he grabbed her by the arms. "Thought you could run away, huh?"

"Stop!" Kanita yelled as she tried to twist from his grasp. "Let me go!"

"You thought you could dishonor me?" he yelled, shaking her. "After taking my gold?"

"The *khong man* is a gift whether I accept your proposal or not!" Kanita yelled back, which was technically true, but it was practically unheard of for a woman to take a *khong man* without accepting a proposal. It was not the honorable thing to do.

"Your father accepted the match," Chakri said. "You are mine now, whether you like it or not."

"I'll never marry you!" Kanita said and she spit in Chakri's face.

Chakri gasped in shock, then he slapped her face. "You thieving slut!"

Safi trumpeted and charged toward them. Chakri cried out in fear, but he grabbed Kanita by the arm and dragged her into the cave.

"Safi!" Kanita screamed.

Chakri pushed Kanita to the ground and straddled her waist, grabbing her wrists.

"I've waited a long time for this," he said, leaning down and breathing his hot breath on her cheek. "You'll be mine one way or another."

Then Chakri screamed as he was pulled off of Kanita. Kanita sat up and saw that Safi had reached into the cave with her trunk, pulling Chakri away from her. Safi grunted as she tossed Chakri aside. He rolled across the ground.

Safi let out a trumpeting, loud enough to shake the trees around them. She lowered her head to charge at Chakri.

"Safi! No!" Kanita screamed as she scrambled to her feet and ran in front of Chakri. "If you kill him, they will all come for you! We need to get out of here!"

Safi groaned and leaned down so Kanita could climb on her back. Then she turned and ran through the forest.

"I'll find you, Kanita!" Chakri screamed at them. "You will be mine!"

Kanita held onto Safi's ears and whimpered. Chakri was crazy! She knew he was weird and creepy, but she never imagined he would go to such lengths to track them. How did he even find them? She had no idea where they were, and they had probably been going in different directions. Even now, were they headed back toward her village? She didn't know!

All she knew was that they had to run. They had to run fast and as far away as possible. Safi could do it. She was strong and didn't need much rest. Kanita was the weak one. The one who was starving. The one who was scared. She was the one Chakri was after. She was the one who was putting Safi in danger. If anything ever happened to Safi, she could never forgive herself.

They had to keep going and stay as far away from other people as possible. Chakri didn't have a dog or anything with him. He couldn't have tracked them himself. Someone must have seen them and told Chakri they were in the area. Maybe the children from the river, or the farmers from the durian grove. Maybe they weren't even far from her home village at all. For all she knew, they could just be going in circles!

Kanita still believed that her plan to go to China was their best hope, but she didn't know how to get there or if they would survive the journey. She was so hungry. But her fear of Chakri was stronger. He wanted *her*, and that chilled her to the bone. She could understand him being upset over the loss of the *khong man*, but he seemed to be only using that as an excuse to claim her. She had a feeling that even if she had left the *khong man* behind, he still would have pursued her. He was obsessed with her and was determined to take her as his wife. She didn't know why, and she didn't care. All she knew was that she could never go back. She would never marry that awful man.

She would rather die.

CHAPTER SEVEN

"Ugh," Kanita groaned as her stomach rumbled. She sat up on Safi's back and her head spun as the sun beat down on her. She had lived in the mountains her whole life, but she had been relatively well-off in her village. Her family was comfortable and respected. She never had to forage for food or worry if they could afford their next meal. She had no idea just how hard life in the jungle could be. And she had never learned the skills for it. She knew that vegetables and beans had to grow wild somewhere, but she didn't know how to look for them. She didn't know how to make a fire to cook the food if she found it. And the very idea of having to kill a bird or rabbit filled her with dread.

The sun was hot. The ground was hard. The mosquitoes bit her constantly. And the sounds! The buzzing and clicking never stopped! She was so miserable, she just wanted to scream!

But what could she do? She couldn't go home and she couldn't go into the villages for help. If she wanted to save Safi, she had to suck it up and survive.

Somehow.

🐘

That evening, after it was already dark, the smell of meat cooking over a fire wafted past Kanita's nose. Her mouth watered. She slid down from Safi and together they crept toward the smell.

They came across a small—yet well adorned—camp. From the dark jungle, Kanita and Safi watched as men in military uniforms sat around a large bonfire chatting, laughing, and cooking chickens.

Kanita licked her lips. She knew she couldn't approach the men. It was too dangerous. But as she looked at the tents, she wondered if she could slip inside and find some food or supplies. But if she were caught, she knew the punishment would be grave.

She saw her chance when the men pulled out a board and some porcelain tokens for a gambling game.

"Come on," she whispered to Safi. They snuck around the camp, looking for a tent with some sort of access. She didn't have a knife or anything else sharp, so she couldn't cut her way in. She had to find another way. She checked the bottom of one of the smaller tents to see if she could crawl underneath, but the canvas was pulled taught.

She was beginning to wonder if she dared to sneak around to the front of one of the tents when she saw that the largest and by far fanciest of the tents had an open flap. Upon closer inspection, she realized that the opening was lined with mesh to keep the bugs out, but the canvas had been rolled up to allow for a breeze, like a window. She peeked in and saw a bed, blankets, pillows, a table with books and writing utensils, a large rug on the floor, and several plates of food!

She ran her hands around the window-like opening, which was mostly tight, but the mesh was secured on the inside with ties. Her fingers were slender, so she was able to reach inside just enough to pull one of the ties, loosening the mesh so she could slip her whole hand and then her arm inside to untie the rest of them. She pushed the mesh away and then motioned for Safi to lift her with her trunk. Safi did so, and Kanita clumsily fell into the tent.

She ran over to the table with the food laid out and grabbed a roti, dipping it into a bowl of red curry, and then sighing audibly as she chewed. It was the most incredibly delicious curry she had ever eaten. She took another roti, slathered the curry on it, and then rolled it up to eat as she looked around the room for things she could use.

She found a sling bag and dumped the contents out on the bed. More books, some papers, and pencils. Things she didn't need. She then went back to the food and put the rest of the roti in the bag, along with some roasted chicken, grilled fish, and some sliced mango.

She took a thin blanket from the bed, wrapping it around her shoulders. She opened a trunk and found some very fine clothes made of high-quality linen and silk. They were boy clothes, but they would have to do. She couldn't keep wearing the same clothes she had run away in.

She was about to go back out the window when she noticed a map hanging on the wall. She looked at it, and she could make out Siam, Burma, and Laos. She saw Chiang Mai in the north and Bangkok in the south, but there was no indication that any of the marks on the map represented where the group was camping right now.

"What are you doing here?" a voice behind her said.

A Girl and Her Elephant

She turned and saw a young man about her age standing there, holding up a knife.

She bolted toward the window, but the boy jumped in her way and waved the knife in front of him.

Safi stuck her trunk through the window and knocked the knife from the boy's hand. Then she grunted and started pushing on the wall of the tent.

"No! Safi!" Kanita said, then she turned to the boy and spoke to him in a harsh whisper. "We won't hurt you. I just needed some food and clothes. Here!" She reached into her pocket and pulled out one of Chakri's gold bracelets. "I can pay for it. Take it. Just let us go."

The boy ran his fingers through his hair as he looked from Safi to Kanita and back to Safi.

"You...you're the girl with the elephant," he said in disbelief.

"What?" Kanita asked.

"The girl who ran away with her elephant," the boy repeated. "The one who didn't want to get married. The daughter of the king's mahout."

Kanita felt her face go hot. This boy, this random stranger in the jungle knew all about her.

"How...how do you know that?" she asked nervously.

"Are you kidding?" he asked with a chuckle. "Everyone is talking about you. The king was furious when he found out you stole the bad omen elephant, the one he thought had been put to death years ago."

"She's not a bad omen elephant," Kanita snapped. "She's my friend!"

"Well, whatever you think, the king wants you caught and the elephant put to death," the boy said.

"What?" Kanita gasped.

"When he found out the elephant was still alive," the

boy explained, "he thought that she must be the cause of all the bad things that have happened over the last few years."

Kanita wasn't sure what bad things he was speaking of. Chiang Mai was far from the capital, and not much had changed there that she had noticed. But she had occasionally overheard her father and the other men talk about the encroaching foreigners and the dangers they posed to all the people of Asia.

"The elephant didn't make the king sign those treaties with the British!" Kanita said.

"Hey, be careful," the boy said. "You are in enough trouble already. Don't add treason to the list."

Kanita went to the window and tossed the bag out of it. "I don't care about treason," she said. "And I don't care about the king! All I care about is getting my elephant safely to China."

"China?" the boy asked, and then he nearly doubled over in laughter. "You're heading to China?"

"Yes," Kanita said, holding her chin high. "Why?"

"Well, for one thing, you're from Chiang Mai," he said. "You've been going in the completely wrong direction."

"What?" she asked, her stomach sinking like a stone as one of her worst fears materialized.

The boy walked over to the map and pointed about halfway between Chiang Mai and Bangkok. "We are about here," he said. "If you had gone the other way, you'd be *in* China right now." Then he laughed again.

Kanita gritted her teeth. "If we turn around, we will be in China in no time."

"I doubt it," the boy said. "Your parents are looking for you. Not to mention the king's men."

And Chakri, Kanita thought.

A Girl and Her Elephant

"Plus, everyone has heard of you," the boy went on. "If anyone sees you, you'll be caught for sure."

Kanita gulped. "Am I caught...now?" she asked, suddenly wondering why the boy hadn't called for the soldiers.

"Nah," the boy said. "You've already done the impossible by running away and surviving for this long. And you've traveled so far! I kind of want to see what you do next."

"I need to get out of Siam," she said, but some of the strength had gone out of her voice. If the north was completely blocked to her, how would she ever get to China?

The boy looked back at the map. "Well, if you keep going south, you'll end up in Bangkok, and then the ocean. That's not good."

"No, it's not," Kanita said, moving next to him.

"But you still have Burma to the west," he said, pointing to the map. "And Laos to the east. There's also Kampuchea to the southeast. And Annam past Kampuchea and Laos."

"But what about the colonizers?" Kanita asked. "Those areas could all be very dangerous."

"They won't know what country you are from if they see you," the boy said. "To them, all of us look the same. Your real problem is going to be the locals. They are going to know you don't belong as soon as they see you."

"So, what should I do?" Kanita asked, surprised she was asking for advice from a stranger.

"What you've been doing, I guess," he said as he flopped onto his bed. "Head west, to Burma. Then stick to the jungle as you make your way north."

"I'll try," she said. "But I don't know the way. When I get in the jungle, I can't tell north from south."

"That's no problem," the boy said as he jumped up and

ran over to the trunk she had been rifling through earlier. He then put something into her hand. "It's a compass. Just hold it flat and it will tell you what direction you are going."

"Wow," she said as she watched the arrow spin. "Thanks." She reached back into her pocket for the bracelet she had offered him earlier and held it up again. "Let me pay you," she said. "I'm not a thief or a beggar. I was just scared of going into the villages for help."

"Keep it," the boy said. "I'm sure you'll need it later on."

"Thanks," she mumbled again. Then she looked to the window and motioned for Safi's trunk. Safi reached in, wrapped her trunk around Kanita's waist, and lifted her out of the window and placed her on the ground. Kanita reached down and picked up the bag with the food and clothes she had tossed out earlier.

"Oh, one more thing," the boy said. He ducked away, but came back a moment later, handing her something.

"What is it?" she asked as she took it.

"Soap," he said with a chuckle as the smile ran away from her face. "You stink."

"You're a jerk," Kanita said. "But...thanks."

"Good luck, elephant girl," he said as he raised the mesh window covering and tied it closed again.

Kanita smiled and held the rose-scented soap her to nose as she walked away. Such soap was quite rare in the jungle and even more expensive. She wondered who the rich boy was, but then she thought it was probably better if she didn't know. The fewer attachments she had, the better. He seemed to genuinely want to help her, but only a fool would defy the king as she had done. If anyone pressed him, it would be in his best interest to reveal what he knew.

She looked down at the compass by the light of the moon and turned until it pointed west, toward Burma. That was the direction she should be going. But if the boy betrayed her, or if someone beat the truth of her whereabouts out of him, then people would know exactly where she was and where she was going. She'd be caught quickly.

She turned and faced east, toward Laos, Annam, and Kampuchea. It would be a much longer trek and she could also get to China that way, but she couldn't shake her fear of the French.

She couldn't go north. People would be combing the jungle looking for her.

To the south was Bangkok—and the king of Siam. Yet another man she needed to stay as far away from as possible.

She was trapped.

CHAPTER EIGHT

*S*afi snorted and started walking south, according to Kanita's compass. Kanita pulled on Safi's tail, but Safi just swished her hand away and kept walking.

"Safi!" Kanita said, running up beside her. "What are you doing? We can't go south! That's toward Bangkok! Toward the king! Didn't you hear what that boy said? The king has ordered you to be put to death!"

Safi grunted and leaned down so Kanita could climb up on her back. Once up, Kanita tugged on Safi's ear to get her to turn around, but Safi continued walking in her southernly direction.

"Safi, we can't—" But Kanita was cut off when she sensed danger. "Do you smell that?" she asked.

Smoke!

And not smoke from the fires of the boy's camp. This fire smelled big.

"We should get out of here," Kanita said, but Safi moaned and headed toward the smoky smell.

Kanita sighed and let Safi do what she was going to do. Who can argue with an elephant?

A Girl and Her Elephant

As they got closer to the smell, she started to hear the sound of someone yelling. Then she heard the terrified bleats of goats.

"Help! My goats!" a woman yelled.

Kanita and Safi were still in the trees, but they could see an elderly woman running from a trough with a bucket of water toward a small barn. She tossed the bucket of water on the fire, but it barely did anything to quench the flames. Kanita had no idea why the woman lived alone out here, or how a fire could have started in a barn, but the sounds of the goats trapped inside tore at her stomach. Against her better judgment, she kicked Safi's side with her heels.

"Let's go!" she said.

Safi let out a trumpeting as she charged from the trees, the earth shaking under her stomping feet.

The woman looked up in shock, or in fright—possibly both—as Safi went to her trough and sucked up all the water with her trunk.

"No!" the woman screamed. "I need it!"

"It's okay," Kanita called down from Safi's back.

Safi then turned toward the small barn and sprayed the water on the fire, dousing most of it. Kanita then jumped down and used the blanket she had taken from the boy and used it to pat out the rest of the flames. She opened the gate and several adult and baby goats ran out, grateful for the fresh air.

Kanita took the bucket from the still startled old woman and walked over to a water pump near the house. She filled the bucket with water and refilled the trough so the goats could drink.

"Th-thank you," the old woman finally stammered. "I don't know what I would have done without you."

"What happened?" Kanita asked.

The woman blushed. "Oh, I'm just an old fool. My son went to trade in the city, so I am here all alone. I thought I heard something and came out to check with my lantern. I tripped, worthless old woman I am, and the hay simply went up like kindling." She sucked in a breath as she started to cry. "I almost lost everything."

Kanita wrapped her arm around the woman. "It was an accident. It could have happened to anyone."

"May Heaven bless and keep you, my dear," the old woman said. "And your elephant! How can I ever repay you?"

Kanita shook her head. "You don't owe us anything. We just happened to be in the area."

"But I must do something," the old woman said. "I will tell everyone about the beautiful girl and her...Is that a *white* elephant?"

Kanita looked over at Safi, who was enjoying the attention from all the little goats crowding around her feet. Even by moonlight, her pale coloring was obvious.

"Actually," Kanita said sheepishly, "it would be better for us if you told no one we were here." She hoped the woman would not ask for further explanation, and she was not disappointed.

The old woman pressed her lips and nodded her head. Kanita pressed her hands together and bowed to the woman in thanks and then headed over to Safi.

"Wait just a moment," the woman said, and she ran back to her house.

Kanita considered simply hopping on Safi's back and running away, but before she could bring herself to do it, the woman came back holding a blanket and a woven bag, which she handed to Kanita.

"You ruined your shawl saving my goats," the woman said. "Take this one."

"I couldn't—" Kanita started to say, but the woman cut her off.

"I insist," she said. "And some goat cheese and fresh bread. Also, some carrots and some dried goat meat. Good for traveling."

Kanita's eyes watered, and she bowed her thanks once again. "It is I who can never thank you," Kanita said. She had been so hungry, so lost, so desolate, and now she had met two kindly people in one night. It was more generosity than she could fathom.

Especially since she had let that little boy drown. She wasn't deserving of such aid when she had refused to help someone else. Her guilt and her gratefulness overwhelmed her and she could not stop herself from weeping.

The old woman took Kanita into her arms, and she felt the weight of Safi's trunk on her shoulder.

"My son will not be back for several days," the old woman said. "Come inside and sleep. It is late and the jungle is very dangerous." She started to lead Kanita toward the house, but Kanita pulled back.

"No," she said. "I...We cannot linger. We must travel on. It...it is too dangerous for us."

The old woman nodded. "I will tell no one that you were here," she said. "But I will let no one speak ill of you in my presence."

Kanita wiped the tears from her face and forced a smile. "You have been too good to me. I hope we will meet again someday, under better circumstances."

"I will pray for you, my child," the woman said.

Kanita went to Safi's side and climbed to her back. Safi

patted several of the goats on their heads as she turned to leave, and the goats seemed to bleat their thanks. They resumed their southwardly direction as Safi returned to the jungle.

"Did you hear what the old woman said?" Kanita asked. "She said that she would not let anyone speak ill of us. That means she has probably heard of us already. People have been saying bad things about us." Which made sense to Kanita. She ran away from her parents, from a marriage, stole her *khong man*, rode away on a condemned elephant, and then refused to help a child in need. Anyone who didn't know her but had only heard these facts would think she was a terrible person.

Maybe she was.

She was so confused right now. She had done bad things, yes, but it had all been in the defense of her friend. To protect Safi. That was the part of the story no one knew. If they knew the truth...

But how could she tell her side of the story? No one would listen to her. They would take Safi away before she had a chance. She couldn't risk trying to change people's minds. She couldn't control other people. She couldn't stop the king from wanting Safi dead. She could only decide what she and Safi would do next.

But Safi kept heading south, toward Bangkok. Toward the king. Toward danger.

The king!

His word was law. The people had no choice but to obey him. Even if Kanita's parents wanted to take her back, they would not be able to protect Safi now that the king knew she was still alive after all these years. The only way to save Safi's life would be for the king to pardon her. Perhaps if she had let Safi save that little boy's life, the king would have heard that Safi was not a bad omen elephant, but a hero. Then he would have pardoned her for sure.

But there was nothing she could do about that now. They couldn't go back; they could only go forward, as Safi was doing now.

"Is that why you are going south, Safi?" Kanita asked. "Are you going to ask the king for a pardon?"

Safi raised her trunk up and rubbed Kanita's face.

"From now on," Kanita said. "We will do all the good we can. We will show the king through our actions that you are not a bad luck elephant, but a good luck one. We will gain the goodwill of the people. The king will have to pardon you."

Kanita leaned forward and laid her head on Safi's. For the first time since she left her village, she felt hopeful.

The next morning, Kanita and Safi found their way to the outskirts of a small village. They watched the villagers from the jungle, looking for an opportunity to offer assistance.

Kanita's heart was in her nose, beating like butterfly wings. She licked her lips. This was the first time in weeks she had even considered approaching someone, and she was terrified of how they would be received.

"Look out!" someone yelled, and then there was a crashing sound.

Safi and Kanita looked toward the shouts and saw that several of the logs that the men had been using to build a new house had tumbled to the ground and were now rolling down the street, running over people and into other buildings.

"Let's go!" Kanita told Safi.

Safi let out a trumpet and put herself into the logs' path, which stopped when they ran into her enormous form. She then used her trunk to start picking up the logs and carrying them back to the house they had fallen from.

Kanita heard several people gasp and then begin to murmur as Safi worked. The men who were building the house seemed surprised at first as Safi started handing them the logs, but then they nodded their thanks.

Once the logs were back in order, an older man—a village elder—approached Safi and Kanita. Kanita jumped down and bowed to the man.

"Thank you for your assistance," the man said. "We know the value of a hardworking elephant but are not blessed to be able to afford them here."

"We were only passing by and heard the crashing sound," Kanita said. "We are glad no one was badly injured."

The man nodded and then looked at her pointedly. "You are the girl who ran away with her elephant, aren't you?"

This time, Kanita did not hang her head in shame, but held her chin up. "I am," she said.

Kanita and the village elder watched as some children ran over to play with Safi, who lifted them up with her trunk one at a time into the air and let them ride on her back.

"They say that the elephant with the mark across her face is a bad omen," the man said.

"You can see the truth of the matter yourself, kun," Kanita dared to say. "Safi is a good elephant, and my one true friend."

"I know how easy it is for children to become attached to animals," the man said. "My own daughter has a little dog who follows her everywhere. She even lets the little beast sleep in her bed. But the time will come when my daughter will become a woman. And a husband will not want to share his bed with a dog."

Kanita did not take offense at the man's words. He was trying to give her kindly advice, as an uncle would to a beloved niece.

"But a good husband would not banish the dog from her side completely," Kanita said. "He would not sentence the dog to death because it is ugly."

The man grimaced and considered her words for a moment as they watched the children and the gentle way the elephant played with them.

"I do not pretend to understand all that you and your elephant have suffered, my child," the man said as he laid a hand on her shoulder. "But I will not add to your burden. You are welcome here, among us. And we will speak well of you to those who will listen."

Kanita folded her hands in front of her and bowed, doing her best to contain her excitement. "Thank you, kun," she said. "That is all we ask."

She then ran to Safi and climbed onto her back, turning her out of the village. The children all groaned in disappointment at the elephant leaving, but they followed Safi and Kanita to the edge of the village, waving and laughing the whole way.

As they went back to the jungle, Kanita's heart was full. It was only a small thing, helping the builders move some logs, but it was a start.

At the next village, Kanita and Safi watched for hours, but no disaster presented an opportunity for Safi to show that she was a good luck elephant. They were about to move on when Kanita saw a woman leading a group of dirty children down the street. The woman and the children stopped walking and then got on their knees and held empty bowls out in front of them. Then, several villagers came over and put food and coins in the bowls. They were beggars, but Kanita had never seen such poverty. Her own village was prosperous, and if any family fell on hard times, the rest of the villagers would band together to help the family in need. These children were dressed in tattered clothes and most had no shoes. They were very thin, as though they did not eat full meals. Kanita needed to find out if there was anything she could do to help, so she emerged from the jungle and walked over to the woman. Safi followed close behind.

As Kanita approached the woman, the children looked up and got very excited when they saw Safi. Like the children in the other village, they could not resist running over and playing with her.

"No, children!" the woman said, trying—and failing—to regain control of them. "That elephant is dangerous."

"Safi is a good elephant," Kanita said, letting the woman watch as Safi let the children ride on her back.

The woman watched nervously as the children ran around, squealing with delight, but she did not stop them.

"Forgive my intrusion," Kanita said. "But why do you look so hungry? Does your village not have enough food? Where is your husband?"

"I have no husband," the woman said. "These are not my children. Well, I love them as my own, but they are orphans. They are children who had nowhere else to go, and I could not turn them away when they asked for help. But I am not rich. I have only a small farm two villages away. I can give the children love and a roof to keep them dry, but sometimes we must beg in order to have enough food."

"You have a generous heart," Kanita said. After recently experiencing her own bout with hunger, she couldn't imagine living her entire life in such a way. Even if the village wanted to help, it would be difficult for them to support so many children for so long. She considered the food in her bag, the cheese and dried goat meat from the old woman. She could part with it. Now that she was feeling braver about entering the villages, she could use her *khong man* to buy herself more food.

Her *khong man*!

She reached into her pocket and pulled out one, then two of the gold bracelets. She handed them to the woman.

"Little sister!" the woman gasped, pushing them back toward Kanita's pocket. "Do not let people see you with such wealth! There are bandits in these woods."

"These are for you," Kanita said, thrusting them back at the woman. "You can use them to buy food for your children. Or buy goats, chickens, and grains and have food for the rest of their lives."

"It is too much," the woman said. "I cannot accept it."

The woman's refusal of the gold only strengthened Kanita's resolve. She opened the woman's hand, placed the bracelets into it, and then closed her fingers around it.

"You must," Kanita said. "Heaven compels me to do this thing for you. We must all do what we can to alleviate the suffering of others. You have done your part by loving these children. Let me do mine by helping you feed them."

The woman fell to her knees and kissed Kanita's hand as she wept. "You—and your elephant—are the answer to my prayers!" she cried.

Kanita gripped the woman's arms and pulled her to her feet. "Please, I am no one. I am a wicked daughter who has done evil things. I am only trying to make amends to the world."

The woman pulled Kanita into her arms and held her in a warm embrace. "We all make mistakes, little sister," she said. "They will not define the whole of your life. You will find peace."

Kanita felt her eyes water. She looked back at Safi and saw that many of the other villagers had gathered around, watching the exchange. They were talking amongst themselves of what they had seen and seemed pleased. Many of the people were smiling and were walking up and taking turns petting Safi. It took Kanita a moment to realize what was happening, but then she understood that the people were touching Safi for good luck! Her plan was working!

The woman thanked Kanita and Safi once again and then gathered up her children so they could make the long journey back to their own village. One of the village elders then approached Kanita and asked her if she would like to stay the night in the village as a guest of honor.

Kanita accepted.

CHAPTER NINE

Kanita had planned on waking up before dawn and slipping out of the village before anyone could try to convince her to stay another day. It was too risky to stay in one place for too long. But she had slept so soundly, so deeply, so peacefully, so much better than she had in weeks, she only awoke when the sun streamed into the room and the tweets of jungle birds filled her ears.

She opened her eyes and looked to the window. Safi's big eye peered back at her.

"Did you sleep as well as I did?" Kanita asked. Safi snuffled and kicked a foot.

Kanita looked around and saw that someone had laid out a fresh set of clothes for her along with a bowl of fruit, a bowl of sweet coconut sticky rice, some steamed buns, and fried patongo. She savored the mango and papayas as she dressed and filled her mouth with so much patongo her cheeks were puffed. On a small table were a brush and long piece of cloth to wrap her hair. She tried to run her fingers through her hair, but they instantly got tangled in such a rat's nest. She realized that she must have looked quite a fright. She slowly began to work the brush through her hair, starting at the tips and working her way up.

She tried to remember the last time she brushed her hair. Actually, it was her mother who had last brushed her hair. It was the night before her father brought Chakri to their home. Her mother had sat on her bed, and she sat on the floor between her mother's knees. Her mother unwound her hair from her topknot and then brushed it with a comb carved from the tusks of an elephant who had died many years before. Even though most of the ivory from the elephants went to the king, sometimes he would reward people—like Kanita's father—for their years of faithful service with ivory.

"Mae," Kanita had groaned. "What's taking so long?"

But her mother did not reply. She only hummed a familiar lullaby as she stroked Kanita's hair over and over again. Kanita enjoyed having her hair brushed, but her mother often took much longer than necessary. Kanita thought her mother enjoyed the ritual of brushing her hair more than she did.

If she had known that would be the last time her mother would brush her hair, she would have been more patient.

As she finally finished combing her hair and tying it up on top of her head, she had to blink to keep tears from forming. She missed her mother and wondered what she must be going through. She wondered if the village elder here would let her send her mother a letter. Just a short one to let her know her daughter was safe.

Kanita collected her items in her bag—along with the fruit and steamed buns—and met Safi at the front of the hut. Safi reached up and ran the tip of her trunk around Kanita's face while Kanita stroked Safi's nose ridges.

A Girl and Her Elephant

"Everything will be okay," Kanita told Safi, and Safi snorted in agreement.

Kanita was feeling rested, full, and looked forward to what the day would bring. So far, her goal of helping people see that Safi was in fact a good luck elephant seemed to be working. She only needed that reputation to grow big enough to reach the king and hopefully change his mind. They still had a lot of work to do.

Some of the villagers who had welcomed them the evening before approached them now. There were not as many as before since it was late enough in the morning that men would be working, women would be tending to their homes, and children would either be helping their parents or attending their lessons. But to the few who had come, Kanita bowed a greeting with her hands pressed together in front of her.

"Thank you for your hospitality," Kanita said, and Safi let out a little trumpet of thanks as well.

"It was our pleasure," an older man said. "Now that young mother will not only be able to feed her children, but provide for them as well thanks to the goats she will be able to buy with the gold you gave her."

"I wish her and her children long, happy lives," Kanita said, her heart swelling. "I am afraid that Safi and I must leave you now. I am sure there are many more people who need our help in this world."

The man nodded and pressed his lips, as though he wanted to say more, but was hesitating. Kanita nodded her thanks one last time and then turned to leave.

"Wait," the man said. Kanita looked at him. "There... there is one more thing. Please, come with me." He motioned for her to follow him.

"I have already stayed too long—" Kanita started to say.

"It will take but a moment," the man said. "Please."

The hairs on Kanita's neck stood on end. Something seemed...odd. She looked at the faces of all those gathered, and they were all smiling. Kanita looked at Safi, who did not seem alarmed or agitated. Kanita thought she must just be feeling paranoid. She should not be rude to the people who had treated her so well. She ignored her gut and followed the villagers.

The man led her to another hut not far from the one she had spent the night in and opened the door for her. It was much darker inside the hut, so, as she stepped inside, she could not see much at first. But then someone stepped toward her.

"Kanita!" her father said as he pulled her into his arms.

Kanita gasped in shock and dropped her bag. She tried to back away, but her father's grip around her was tight. She looked back at the door, and the villagers were still smiling, some wiping tears from their eyes as they closed the door. They must have thought they were observing some tender reunion. But in truth, all Kanita wanted to do was run away.

She could hear Safi snuffling and stomping her feet in agitation at not being able to see her. Safi moved from the door and around the building until she found a small window. When she saw Kanita's father, her trumpeting and foot stomping became more pronounced.

"P-Por!" Kanita stammered, then she looked to the window. "Safi! It...it's okay...I think..."

"You are alive!" her father cried, holding her tight again. "Your mother and I were so worried about you."

Kanita started to relax a little, but she still felt uncomfortable. She couldn't remember a time in her life when her father showed her such affection.

A Girl and Her Elephant

"I'm sorry," she said. "I wanted to let you know I was safe, but I was so scared."

"I know," her father said, pulling back a little but still holding tightly to her forearms. "I was very angry at you. But at the thought of losing you, I had to get you back. Word of you reached my ears even in the north. I traveled so far, asking every person I met if they had seen you. They finally led me here."

Kanita sighed, a feeling of relief washing over her. Her father understood why she ran away! Maybe he would forgive her.

"Oh Por!" she said, leaning into his chest, and he hugged her once again. "How is Mae?"

She thought she felt her father tense at the mention of her mother, but then he said, "She's fine. She is worried too." But the warmth had fled his voice.

Kanita looked up at her father's face. Even though he didn't look angry, there was something behind his eyes. Irritation? Guilt? She wasn't sure. What wasn't he telling her about her mother? Was she sick? Did she also run away?

Did he beat her?

They looked at each other in silence for a moment. Kanita was almost afraid to say anything lest it lead to another fight. She still could not go back. She could never marry Chakri. And she still had to save Safi. Her father coming to find her had not changed anything.

"Your mother and I," her father finally said evenly, "want you to come home."

She took a moment to consider her response before replying. "I know," she said, stepping away from him. "But unless something has changed—"

"Everything has changed," her father said. "I am no

longer the king's mahout. He fired me when he learned what happened."

"I'm sorry," Kanita said. Even though she feared he would be punished for her actions, to hear that it had come to pass sent a shock through her.

"It's my fault," her father said to her surprise. "I should have obeyed the king in all matters from the beginning."

Kanita gulped and took another step back. She knew he was referring to killing Safi when he had first been ordered to.

"But I cannot change the past," her father said. "I must try to make everything right now. And that will start by bringing you home."

"What about Safi?" she asked.

"Safi will come with you," he said.

"Really?" she asked, her voice cracking.

"The elephant is no longer a baby, but is full grown," her father said. "She is a cherished pet and look at all the good she has been doing."

Kanita nodded, her eyes watering. She could not speak for fear the tears would flow over. Her father understood why Safi was so important to her and saw the good works they had been doing to try and save her.

"Come back home, Kanita," her father said. "And bring Safi with you. I will fix everything."

"Por!" she said, hugging him again. He patted her on the head.

"Let us leave this place," he said, reaching for her bag.

"But, what about Chakri?" Kanita asked.

Her father was no longer smiling. "What about him?"

"I...I can't marry him," she said. "He is a cruel man. He will hurt me if he sees me again."

"I will...deal with Chakri when we return," her father said. But that wasn't enough for Kanita.

"Tell me you won't force me to marry him," Kanita said. "Or I won't go back."

Her father grimaced and looked away. She thought he was going to lose his temper, as she had seen him do so many times.

"I will not force you to marry Chakri," he finally said. He picked up a large bag off the floor. He must have brought plenty of food and clothes with him for the journey. He had probably been looking for her for weeks. Then he walked to the door an opened it. He extended his arm to her, expecting her to walk out by his side.

Kanita was torn. She wanted to believe her father. She wanted to go home. She missed her mother. She *worried* about her mother. She needed to make sure her mother was safe.

But could she trust the word of her father? She felt like a wicked child for even thinking such a thought. A child should always trust and obey their parents. For her father to even be here, practically begging for her to return home with him took great humility on his part. She was ashamed at having humiliated her father in such away.

And she had cost him his job! What would he do now? What would they all do? How would they have food and clothes and firewood? She started to feel afraid of what she had done. She had been so foolish to think that by running away her life would change but her parents' life would remain the same. Of course the king would punish her father. Not to mention the embarrassment she must have caused her father among the other villagers. A man who could not even control his own daughter! He was right to be angry with her.

Yet here he was, offering her everything she wanted. Everything she needed. She could go home. She could see her mother again. He would help her save Safi's life. And she wouldn't have to marry that despicable Chakri. And together, she could help restore her father's reputation. Maybe even his position. After all, if the king accepted Safi as a good luck elephant, he would have to give her father his job back.

Everything would be fine.

At the window, Safi paced anxiously. Kanita understood how she felt. She was ready to go home too. She reached out and took her bag from her father's hand and slung it over her shoulder.

Kanita took her father's hand and, together, they left the hut.

CHAPTER TEN

As Kanita emerged back into the sunlight, her father holding her hand so tightly he restricted the blood flow, the villagers cheered. Kanita tried to smile, but her mouth couldn't quite complete the task. She knew she was doing the right thing, but she was scared at the same time. She wanted to believe her father, but doubt nagged at the back of her mind.

Safi came around the side of the building and wrapped her trunk around Kanita's wrist. Kanita wrested her other hand away from her father and patted Safi's nose.

"It's okay," she said. "We are going home."

Safi grunted and pulled Kanita away from her father.

Her father frowned and took Kanita's hand back in his. "This way," he said, pulling her through the crowd.

The elderly villager who had brought Kanita to her father in the first place approached them and patted her father on the shoulder.

"I am glad to see you and your daughter have made amends," the man said.

"It is still a long road ahead," her father said, and Kanita agreed silently. Even if she went home with him and everything was as he said it would be, it would be a long time before she ever fully trusted him again, if ever.

"Perhaps you should stay and share a meal with us," the man said. "Fortify you for the journey ahead."

"We should be on our way," her father said, still pulling Kanita along. She wondered why he was being so rude to the man. Even though he did not know the man well, he was her father's elder as well and he should show him respect.

Safi was following along, but very slowly, and she still held Kanita's other hand in her trunk. Kanita felt her arms being stretched between her father and her elephant.

"Come on, Safi," Kanita said over her shoulder, but her words seemed to have the opposite effect.

Safi grunted and stopped. Kanita cried out in pain as her father tried to keep walking but stumbled backward.

"What the devil?" her father asked, looking from her to the elephant, his brow furrowed.

"Safi," Kanita hissed. She could feel her own anxiety rising at the thought of making her father angry. "Come on. We are going home."

Safi groaned and took a step back, dragging Kanita and her father with her.

"You stupid beast!" her father yelled as he stepped toward Safi, his fist raised.

Safi trumpeted and stepped to the side, away from Kanita's father.

"Por!" Kanita said. "She's just scared." She ripped her hand from her father again and ran her hand up the side of Safi's face. "It's okay girl. He's changed. He won't let anyone hurt you."

A Girl and Her Elephant

Her father pushed her aside and pulled his ankusha out of his bag, raising it high. Kanita's eyes went wide and her heart sank into her stomach. She hadn't realized he had brought the dreaded training hook with him.

"It's about time someone trained you properly, Safi!" he yelled as he swung the hook down, stabbing Safi in the back of her foot.

"Por!" Kanita screamed, but it was too late.

Safi cried out in pain and reared up on her back legs, letting out a trumpet loud enough to shake the trees.

Even though many mahouts used the ankusha to train their elephants, Kanita had never even considered using one on Safi. She had used only positive training techniques, like rewards for good behavior, instead of punishing her for making mistakes.

"Get down, monster!" her father yelled, using a voice that usually cowed his own elephants, but was one Safi was not used to.

Safi's front feet thudded back to the ground. She snorted and lowered her head.

"Going to charge me, are you?" her father asked. He reached into his bag and pulled out his rifle. One used especially for killing elephants. The same one he had pointed at Safi eight years before.

"Por!" Kanita cried. "Stop! What are you doing?"

"I was going to wait until we were out of the village before doing this," he said as he raised the gun to his shoulder to take aim. "But I might as well do it now."

"What?" Kanta cried, her mind swimming. She ran over and grabbed her father's shoulder, pulling his gun down from his face. "What is happening?"

"It's the only way, Kanita," he said shaking her off. "The

only way to appease the king and get my job back. He wants her head on a platter." He raised the gun again.

She looked back at his bag and saw a bit of rope. He had lied to her! He had planned to kill Safi all along and then tie her up and drag her back home kicking and screaming. Was he still planning to marry her off to Chakri as well?

"No!" Kanita said, jumping up and grabbing at the gun barrel with her bare hands. "I won't let you!"

Her father swung his arm, his elbow hitting Kanita in the jaw. She lost her grip on the gun, enabling him to push her to the ground.

"Stay down, child," he ordered. "*I* am the parent, and you will obey me—"

He screamed as Safi's trunk slammed into his side, throwing him to the edge of the village and into a tree.

Safi trumpeted and gently picked up Kanita in her trunk and placed her up on her back. Then she turned and charged out of the village, the villagers screaming and yelling, waving their arms, trying to get her to stop.

But Safi would not stop. She ran as fast as she could.

Kanita was in a daze, both from her father hitting her and from the truth she had just learned. She looked back and saw the villagers crowding around her father. She saw him raise his head and look at her.

At least he wasn't dead.

But she was probably dead to him. She lowered her head and cried as Safi entered the jungle, smashing through everything in her path.

"Oh Por…Por!" Kanita cried. She had known that it was too much to hope for, that her father would take her—and Safi—back home with open arms. But he had been so warm, so loving. He had shown her more affection in those few minutes than he had shown her in her entire life. For just a moment, she wanted to believe that he loved her and would put her needs first.

But it was too much to ask. Too much to hope for. Her father was not only going to kill Safi, but he was going to shoot her right in front of her! And then he was going to ship her head to the king! He had called Safi a monster, but it was her father who was the monster. Who knew what evil that man was capable of. Just what would have happened if she had gone home with him? He would have beaten her for sure. Then he would have given her to Chakri, who would have beaten her as well. But not just once—for the rest of her life.

And what of her poor mother. Her heart felt ripped in two. How her mother must be suffering right now. She wanted so much to turn Safi north, to go to Chiang Mai and rescue her mother from her father. Together, they could find freedom.

But she couldn't. According to what she had learned, people all over the north were looking for her. Anyone might try to capture her and give her back to her father.

And what about Safi? Safi was already wanted by the king, but now there would be an order sent out. She had injured a human. A mahout. She would now be branded as a rogue elephant. And there was only one sentence for a rogue elephant, one too dangerous to let live.

Safi would be killed on sight.

Kanita felt sick to her stomach. She had ruined everything. She never should have stayed in the village. She should have left as soon as she gave the woman the gold. When she saw her father, she should have run! Safi had been agitated as soon as she saw Por. She knew he was dangerous. Kanita should have listened. She should have run out of that hut and never looked back.

But now it was too late. Kanita and Safi were both in danger.

And there was no one they could turn to for help.

CHAPTER ELEVEN

Safi kept running while Kanita wept. She couldn't believe her own father had betrayed her like that! And Safi! Oh, Safi. She knew that Safi loved her and was only trying to protect her, but to attack her father. It was foolish. No, it was stupid. It wasn't like with Chakri. Chakri was dangerous. He was going to hurt her. Rape her. Safi had saved her. And that had been in the jungle with no one else to see what happened. Safi had attacked her father in broad daylight in front of an entire village, and the goodwill Safi had built up with the villagers was now gone. No one would trust them now.

Kanita didn't know how word about them was traveling so quickly, but she was certain the rest of the villages would learn about the girl with the dangerous elephant soon enough. They wouldn't be allowed in. No one would let them help or offer their assistance. They would be run out of town at best, and Safi would be shot on sight at worst.

Kanita sat up and patted Safi on the head. "Safi," she cooed. "You need to slow down. We need to decide what to do next."

Safi moaned as she slowed from a run to a trot, and then to a walk. Kanita sighed with relief as she stretched her arms over her head. All of the tension that had eased during her restful night of sleep had returned with a vengeance. She opened her bag and pulled out the goat cheese and roti bread.

The sharp, tangy flavor of the goat cheese comforted her and reminded her of her mother cooking in their kitchen back home. That was why her father's betrayal had hurt so much. She *wanted* to go home. She didn't want to seek out the king. She was just a simple girl from a rural mountain village. All she had ever wanted was to train her elephant and one day be a mahout like her father.

But even that simple dream was impossible. Her father had told her many times that only boys could be mahouts. She had hoped that by learning the ways of a mahout on her own, and by proving herself through training Safi, her father would eventually see that she was as capable as any boy of being a mahout and would accept her.

She had always been foolish. In the back of her mind, she knew her father would never accept her and she would have to marry and have children and live a life like every other woman in the village. But she hadn't been ready for that when her father presented her to Chakri. How could he not see that? It was as if her father—despite her attempts to please him—had never seen *her* at all. It was clear he didn't know who she was as a person.

It was as if she had been a doll. One he wanted to dress and perform the way *he* wanted her to. And when she didn't work the way he thought she should, he threw her to the ground and stomped away. If she wasn't going to comply with his wishes, he didn't want her in his life. Even if that meant marrying her off far too young to an old, cruel man.

Safi ambled through the brush, grabbing leaves and grass to eat as they wandered aimlessly. Kanita reached into her bag and pulled out the compass. She was not surprised to see that they were heading south. She had no idea why Safi was intent on traveling in this direction, but she had come to expect it.

"Safi," Kanita moaned as she put her things back into her bag. "Why are you going this way? Do you know something I don't?"

Safi grunted and lifted her trunk to Kanita's face. Kanita let Safi pet and sniff her and then kissed the tip of her trunk.

"I wish you could tell me what you are thinking," Kanita said with a sigh.

They came across a narrow river, and Safi walked right into it.

"Safi!" Kanita cried, tossing her bag on the shore as they went in the river and Safi rolled over on her side. Kanita jumped off of Safi and ended up in waist deep water. She completely submerged herself, letting the cool water wash over her. She stood up and saw that Safi was spraying herself with the water. Not for the first time, she wished she had an elephant brush with her. She went over to Safi's stomach and ran her hands over her, trying to break up as much of the caked-on dirt as she could.

Safi filled her trunk with water and sprayed it at Kanita. Kanita squealed with laughter as she ran to Safi's head and splashed water at her face. Safi slapped her trunk in the water, causing a small wave that knocked Kanita off her feet.

For a few minutes, they played in the water and forgot their troubles.

After they were washed and done playing, they crawled to the shore and let the sun's afternoon rays dry them off.

They listened to the sounds of the jungle, the birds tweeting, the bugs chirping. It didn't sound quite so scary anymore. If only they could just live here in the jungle by themselves forever. No one to bother them. No one to threaten them. No one to hurt them or try to separate them.

But Siam was not an island. Eventually, they would be found. And Safi, with her pale color and bright red birthmark, would always be instantly recognized.

"What are we going to do, Safi?" Kanita asked. "We can't just keep running. We have to have a plan."

Safi wrapped her trunk around Kanita's shoulders and grunted. Kanita sighed.

"Our best hope for getting protection for you is still the king," Kanita admitted. "He was the person who ordered for you to be put to the death in the first place. Only he can cancel that order."

Kanita thought about how the king had actually ordered Safi's death many years ago, back when she had been born, but the people of her village ignored him. If only they could have kept living in such peace and protection.

She shook her head. No point in dreaming about what might have been.

"We still need to find a way to get you into the good graces of the king," Kanita said. "I suppose that helping people would still be the best approach. We could never have hoped to go to Bangkok and see the king ourselves, but it will be even more dangerous to try now. If people hear what happened to Por..." She didn't want to finish that sentence. She didn't want to think about the look on her father's face when Safi attacked him. She didn't want to imagine that Safi really had it in her to hurt someone.

"Come on," Kanita said, standing up and dusting her butt off. She crawled up Safi's side and then made her way up Safi's back as Safi stood. "We need to keep going. We can't stay in one place too long. We will have to be careful, but we can still help people. We can still try to get people to see that you are not a rogue elephant."

It was a long shot. It was foolish and dangerous and would probably lead to one or both of them getting killed, but there was nothing else they could do. They had to keep going.

As they walked through the jungle, Kanita marveled —not for the first time—at how quietly Safi, and all elephants, were able to navigate a forest. An elephant could walk right up behind you and you would never hear it. It was how they had been able to sneak up to and observe so many villages undetected. Even someone as small as Kanita would make a racket compared to the natural stealth of an elephant.

The village they approached now was no different. Safi and Kanita stood in the shaded shelter of the trees and watched the people going about their daily lives. But these villagers seemed busier than the others they had approached. Busier, yet not seeming to do anything more than talk. As husbands arrived home from working in the jungle or nearby villages, wives came out of their homes to tend their goats and chickens, and children enjoyed a short break before dinner and evening chores, people who had already gathered outside would rush to greet the new arrivals and talk with great animation, their arms waving and their eyes and mouths big.

What were the people so excited about? For a moment, Kanita had a sinking feeling the story of the girl with the bad luck rogue elephant had already reached the village. And yet, there was something about the villagers' mannerisms that told her the people weren't talking about her and the elephant. If there were a rogue elephant on the loose, people would be acting more afraid. They would make sure their animals were secure and they wouldn't let their children run free. Men with guns would be situated around the perimeter of the village to keep the rogue elephant from attacking the people. But if they weren't concerned about a rogue elephant, what *was* going on?

Kanita would have to get closer to find out what everyone was talking about. She thought it likely that the village had not yet heard about the rogue elephant. It was possible that they still thought Safi was, in fact, the good-luck elephant who had been helping in the area. Kanita took a deep breath and stepped out of the trees and into the village, Safi right behind her.

As soon as she came into view, she could hear a collective gasp as everyone looked at them. But no one screamed. No one ran. No one drew their gun. After the initial shock wore off, the children of the village burst into laughter as they ran toward the lucky white elephant.

"Pick me! Pick me!" the children chanted as they ran around Safi, hoping she would pick them up and put them on her back. Safi's steps slowed as she played with the children, but Kanita moved closer to where the adults had gathered and greeted them with her hands folded.

"You must be the girl with the good luck elephant that was once a bad luck elephant," one of the older women said with a smirk.

"I suppose," Kanita said. "It is hard to tell what reputation we will have with each village we enter."

"You should go home to your mother," another woman chided harshly.

Kanita's heart stopped and her smile left her face. "Yes, auntie," she said. "I wish I could."

"Sama!" the first woman hissed, slapping the second woman on the arm. "Do not be so harsh. You do not know her struggle."

The woman hmphed and crossed her arms.

"Ignore her," the woman said to Kanita. "Of course, there is truth in her words. We all wish to see you safely home. But I know no young girl would have undertaken such a harsh journey if she had any other choice."

"Thank you," Kanita said. "I am only trying to protect my elephant."

The woman nodded. "What has brought you here?"

"We are looking for opportunities to do good and help people in need," Kanita said.

"Maybe the girl and her elephant should rescue the prince," a man quipped, and everyone else laughed.

"Prince?" Kanita asked, cocking her head.

"The king's eldest son, the Crown Prince Mongkut," the elderly woman said. "He was on a hunting expedition and kidnapped by rebels."

"That sounds terrible," Kanita said.

"Not just any rebel," someone else added. "Decha. He has been tormenting the king for years. His tribe of bandits has grown powerful. They killed the prince's men."

"The prince is lucky to be alive," someone else said. "Decha hates the king."

"Why?" Kanita asked.

"It doesn't matter," another person answered. "The king is appointed by Heaven. To rebel is a sin!"

Kanita didn't reply to that. She understood the sentiment and agreed that people should obey the king as far as they are able. But she had also once agreed that children should obey their parents. She now knew that there could be extreme circumstances that might cause a child to disobey. The same could be true of a king's subjects.

She had no idea if this Decha had just cause for his rebellion or not, but if she and Safi were to save Prince Mongkut's life, surely he would pardon Safi!

"Where are the king's men now?" Kanita asked. "The guards and soldiers. Are they looking for the prince?"

"Of course," the elderly woman said. "But we have heard they are having a terrible time trying to penetrate the forest. Decha and his men have retreated to the Atid Ridge across the Songkran River. It is too thick and dangerous for an army to get through."

"And no one knows the jungle like Decha," someone added. "If he wants to remain hidden, the king will never find him."

"Where is this Atid Ridge?" Kanita asked.

"East of here," the elderly woman said. "But take heed, child. You are not really considering going after the prince, are you? It is too dangerous."

Probably not as dangerous as staying here once you find out Safi is a rogue elephant, Kanita thought. She smiled and shook her head. "I was only curious as to where we were. We have been wandering for weeks."

The woman nodded, but her eyes showed that she did not believe Kanita's words. Still, she did not try to stop her from leaving. Instead, the woman ordered the others to collect food, clothes, and some other supplies for Kanita and sent her on her way with a blessing.

"May Heaven protect you, little one," she said.

A Girl and Her Elephant

"Thank you for your help," Kanita said, and everyone sent her and her elephant off with a wave and a smile.

Kanita and Safi left the village and took a trail heading south. But as soon as the village was out of view, Kanita pulled out her compass and urged Safi to the east.

"Come on, Safi," Kanita said. "I know you want to go south to see the king, but the king's son is to the east. If you want a pardon, that is the way we need to go."

Safi grunted, but then she turned to the east. Toward the rebel's camp.

CHAPTER TWELVE

It was already evening by the time Kanita and Safi left the village, so they decided to sleep in the woods that night. Kanita could not risk her father finding her in another village. Kanita did not find another outcropping to sleep under, but this time she had several shawls and blankets she had been given along the way, so she was able to spread a blanket out over a patch of crinum lilies and make a rather soft bed for herself. She covered herself with one shawl and made a small pillow out of another. Nearby, Safi leaned against a tree. Kanita had enough food in her bag that she did not go to bed hungry. Had she not been so anxious about finding the prince, she would have slept quite comfortably.

Kanita packed up and hopped on Safi's back to set off for the rebel camp as soon as the sun started to rise feeling excited and hopeful. It was the perfect plan. If they found the camp, Safi could sneak Kanita close enough that she could find the prince. Then, she would slip into the camp undetected, release the prince, and Safi would get them back to Bangkok before the rebels even knew the prince was gone! The king would pardon Safi, maybe even give Kanita a reward for rescuing the prince, and Kanita could then return home and beg her father for forgiveness. Surely, after everything she had been through, her father would take her back. He would still be angry at her, of course, as she was still angry with him, but they were family. They loved each other. One way or another, she would find her way back home.

For the most part, even though Kanita and Safi had been avoiding main roads and villages, they had followed paths through the jungles previously forged by humans, elephants, and other animals. The part of Siam they had been exploring was rather well-populated, with villages located every few miles.

But here, the further east they traveled, was a far less hospitable part of the country. The trees were so thick, even Safi had a hard time finding a way through. They often had to retrace their steps to try and find another way through the brush, around small mountains, or into valleys and back up again. It was very slow-going. Even though Kanita had her compass, she often thought they were only walking in circles, covering the same ground over and over again. Safi even grew frustrated, groaning and hesitating when Kanita gave her orders.

By that night, Kanita guessed that they had not traveled very far at all, but they were both exhausted. Kanita, at least, still had food to eat, but the ground was hard and the mosquitoes were thick. The sounds of the jungle were loud here. The incessant clicking and hooting—not to mention her itching arms and legs—prevented her from getting any sleep.

The next morning, Kanita and Safi set off once again, but this time they were exhausted, thirsty, and grumpy.

They had not come across a stream at all the day before. At least this day it felt like they were making a little more progress. There were still rocks and thick trees blocking their path in many places, but according to Kanita's compass, they backtracked far less often and were generally heading in the right direction—albeit slowly.

By about midday, the trees seemed to get a little more sparse as the sun beat down on them.

"I think we might be going uphill," Kanita observed. "That might be why we have had such a hard go of it. They did say that Atid was a ridge, which would mean it is part of a mountain range. The rivers will be down below us, so that's why we haven't found water."

Safi snuffed her annoyance. Discovering the truth of their situation didn't make it any more tolerable.

"I'm sorry, Safi," Kanita said. "Don't be angry with me. I couldn't stand it if you were angry with me as well."

Safi groaned and rubbed her trunk over Kanita's face.

"I love you too, Safi," Kanita said, giving the top of her head a kiss.

Suddenly, Safi stopped.

"Come on, girl," Kanita urged, but Safi didn't budge. She only let out a low gurgling sound. "What is it?" Kanita asked, looking around. She didn't see anything, but she didn't hear anything either. That was when she realized she didn't hear *anything*. No birds, no monkeys, no insects. It was even more unsettling than the constant jungle noises that kept her awake at night.

Kanita gulped. Were they near the rebel camp? Had the rebels hunted the area completely clean?

"We have to keep going," Kanita whispered. "The rebels could be close."

Safi grunted and took a step backward.

A Girl and Her Elephant

"Ugh, no!" Kanita said as she jumped down. She knew that if she walked, Safi would follow, even if it was against Safi's better judgment.

Kanita headed forward, moving vines and large leaves out of her way. As she knew she would, Safi followed, but at a distance.

"Come on!" Kanita said. "It's fine. See?"

Kanita took another step forward and then screamed as she slipped down an embankment. The hillside was damp and so steep she couldn't stop herself from tumbling head over heels. She finally slammed into the ground below, landing on her shoulder with such a force she was afraid she had dislocated it. She moaned as she sat up. Despite the pain, she forced her arm to move. Thankfully it did, so it wasn't broken or dislocated.

"Safi!" she yelled up the hill. Safi trumpeted back. Kanita could tell the elephant was frightened. "I...I'm okay. Just...just try to find a way down." She was already incredibly sore. Her back hurt and her legs were bruised. She knew she would not be able to climb back up the way she came. She would have to find another way to meet Safi.

She forced herself into standing position and looked around. She was deep in the brush, but in something like a grotto. The area was a bit open, as if someone had walked the area often, smashing down the vegetation.

Someone...or some*thing*!

Her heart started to race as she realized she must be near the den of a large predator.

Don't panic. Don't panic. Don't panic, she repeated to herself. *Most predators are just as scared of me as I am of them, right?*

She went through the list of possibilities in her head. What could be living in such an inhospitable area? A tiger?

A bear? Whatever it was, nothing attacked elephants. As long as Safi got to her in time, she'd be fine, right?

But then she heard it—that distinctive low hissing growl. Her blood ran cold. It was right behind her.

She broke out into a sweat and slowly turned around. Right in front of her stood the largest king cobra she had ever seen in her life. It hissed at her again, its fangs bared and its black hood flared.

Kanita felt her mouth go dry and knew that she was about to lose her bladder. Cobras were usually solitary creatures, but she had invaded the cobra's home and it would attack to defend its territory.

Its territory! That's why the jungle had been so quiet. Cobras were highly territorial. This one would have killed or run off anything it didn't want near its home.

The cobra stared her down, continuing to hiss and growl at her. She wanted to flee, but she knew that any sudden movement might startle the creature and cause it to attack. She should attempt to back away slowly but was too scared. Her feet were stuck to the ground.

The ground began to shake. And before Kanita or the cobra could react, Safi stomped into the den and let out a ferocious trumpeting.

The cobra turned to Safi and snapped at her in self-defense, but Safi slapped at the cobra with her trunk, hurling it toward the back of the den. Kanita ran to Safi and scampered up her side to her back. Safi immediately turned and ran back the way she came. Kanita looked back and saw the snake slither away, back into the dark as they fled.

Kanita leaned down and wrapped her arms around Safi's neck and kissed the back of her head.

"Oh, thank you! Thank you!" she said. She had never in

her life been more terrified. Even Chakri had not made her bowels turn to jelly like that.

Safi kept running, so Kanita pulled out her compass to see which direction they were going. She was pleased to see they were heading east! Somehow, Safi had found a break in the jungle and they were finally gaining ground.

"We are going to make it, Safi!" Kanita cried out as the trees parted and they found the sun once again. The birds were singing and the monkeys were chattering. Surely, their journey was about to come to an end.

For quite a while, Kanita had suspected they were going uphill. It had been gradual, not like climbing a mountain, but slowly they had been moving up in elevation.

Kanita's suspicions were confirmed when the ground suddenly came to an end, and they found themselves looking straight down a cliff at a rushing river far below.

"You have got to be kidding me!" Kanita cried. They looked left and right, but she could not see any way to cross to the other side, which was so far away, no human or animal could jump it.

"What did the old woman say?" Kanita asked. "That Atid Ridge was on the other side of the Songkran River. This must be the Songkran. If the rebel camp is on the other side, that means there must be a way across."

Safi moaned.

"Come on, girl," Kanita said. "Don't lose hope. We are going the right way. We will find the prince. We just have to find the way across."

Kanita looked back and forth again, hoping to see a way down the cliffside or a bridge or something. Somehow the rebels were crossing the river. They just had to find the same path.

"Well," Kanita said. "Left or right? You choose."

Safi lifted her trunk and sniffed the air. Then she turned to the left.

Kanita patted Safi's head. "Good girl, Safi," she said. "I'm sure you know what you are doing."

Safi didn't reply, but slowly walked along the edge of the cliff in the direction she had chosen.

They hadn't walked far when they crested a small rise. When Kanita looked down, she saw a bridge!

"Safi!" Kanita cried. "You found it!"

Safi ambled toward the bridge, and Kanita's hopes sank as she got a better look at it. The bridge was mostly made of rope that tied wooden planks together for walking across. It wasn't the most rickety bridge in the world, but it certainly had not been made with elephants in mind.

Kanita slid down and stepped onto the bridge. It held her easily. The ropes were woven together and the wooden planks were new. She suspected that the rebels had only constructed the bridge recently. She jumped up and down, and the bridge only lightly swayed.

"I think...I think the bridge is solid," she said to Safi. Safi groaned and took a step back. "I can't rescue the prince without you, Safi. If you don't go, there is no point in me going alone."

Safi let out a small honk and put one foot on the bridge. The bridge creaked, and Safi stepped back. Kanita walked further out onto the bridge, about a third of the way.

"Come on!" she called back. "It's okay!"

Safi stepped out with one foot, then another. Kanita held her breath. The bridge bowed, but it didn't break. Safi took another step forward, and then another, putting all her weight on the bridge. The bridge sagged a bit more, but it held.

Kanita blew out the breath she had been holding.

A Girl and Her Elephant

"Great!" she called out, waving Safi forward. "Come on. We should go as quickly as possible!"

Safi stepped forward cautiously, and Kanita walked backward, never taking her eyes off Safi and urging her forward. She took slow steps, letting Safi catch up with her until they were together about halfway across the bridge.

"See!" Kanita said, placing her hand on Safi's trunk. "Now is the easy—"

They heard a loud crack! The bridge shuddered.

Kanita looked ahead and saw that the ropes holding the bridge to the edge of the cliff were giving way.

"Run!" Kanita said, but it was too late. One of the ropes ahead of them snapped. "Back up!" she screamed. "Back to the other side!"

Safi stepped back quickly, but the board under her foot collapsed under her, causing her weight to shift and the bridge to swing. There was a loud groaning sound and the whole bridge buckled beneath them.

"Hurry! Go!" Kanita said as she tried to pull herself forward, but the collapsing bridge and Safi's weight created an incline Kanita had to climb up as opposed to run across.

They would never make it to the other side in time.

Kanita looked back, but the boards under Safi's feet were splintering one by one.

They were going to die.

"Safi!" Kanita cried. "I'm sorry!" She gripped the rope and closed her eyes, expecting to fall at any second.

Instead, she felt herself flying. She opened her eyes just as Safi used all of her strength to propel Kanita to the far side of the bridge. She landed on the wooden planks hard on her knees but within reach of the grass on the other side. She scrambled to her feet and looked back.

"Safi!" she screamed, "Run!" But Safi couldn't move. She

let out a strangled trumpet as the last of the ropes snapped and the bridge collapsed.

Kanita could only watch as Safi—her elephant, her best friend—fell into the rushing river below.

"Safi! Safi!" she screamed over and over again. But she never saw Safi surface.

Kanita had no idea how long she watched the river flow below her as she cried and screamed Safi's name. But by the time her voice no longer worked, it was too dark to see the water below. Kanita finally dragged herself away from the cliff's edge and leaned against a tree where she cried long into the night.

CHAPTER THIRTEEN

Kanita sat up, shocked she had fallen asleep at all. She must have exhausted herself at some point and passed out. Shaking, she crept to the edge of the cliff and peeked over the edge. Against all hope, she prayed she might somehow see Safi at the bottom in the morning light.

"Safi?" she called out. But she heard and saw nothing other than the water flowing through the ravine below. She looked down river until it disappeared around a bend, but she did not see her precious elephant.

Even though elephants could swim, she wasn't sure Safi would have survived the fall, especially if the river was not particularly deep. It was swift-moving, but she could not see how deep or shallow it was from such a distance. The river could pose other dangers as well. She knew that crocodiles inhabited many of Siam's rivers. She couldn't see any from the top of the cliff, but there could be some under the water, blending in with the rocks, or further downstream. The chance that Safi survived would be minuscule at best.

Kanita leaned on one hand as she sat on the grass in the

rising sun. What was she going to do now? The remains of the bridge dangling down the side of the cliff clattered in the breeze, taunting her. This whole misadventure had been to save Safi's life, and now Safi was gone. And it was all her fault. She had been in such a hurry to find the bandits and rescue the prince, she hadn't waited to find a safer way to cross the river. Safi had trusted her. The guilt gnawed at her stomach, making her ill.

She didn't think she could go home. She had run away, disobeyed her parents, and stolen her *khong man*. She was a disgrace. She had also allowed Safi to attack her father. She knew he had lived, but how badly had he been injured? She had also cost him his job and his reputation. She had ruined her father's life. And she had done nothing to redeem herself. Her elephant was dead and she had not rescued the prince. There was no reason why her father should accept her back. She imagined that her mother would still want her to come home, but her mother would have no say in the situation. She would have to obey her husband. And if she went home, with no job, how would her parents have food for themselves? Much less for a worthless daughter. She would only be a burden to them. Their only option would be to find her a husband to accept her. But what man would be that foolish? No one would want the girl who was the ruin of her family.

Maybe she could join a temple and become a nun. She could dedicate herself to Guanyin, the Goddess of Mercy, and spend the rest of her life atoning for her sins. Though, she had never heard of a girl being allowed to become a nun. Boys were allowed to become monks, but the only nuns she knew of were old women who were widows, and most had no children or grandchildren. Girls were expected to marry, not cut themselves off from civilization. Still, she would stop at every temple she came across and beg them to accept her. She didn't know what else to do.

She stood up and looked at the remnants of the bridge. She couldn't get back to the other side here. She would have to find another way back across. She didn't want to keep heading east on her own. If the bandits caught her, they would probably deal badly with her. And she didn't want to end up in Annam or Laos. No, she needed to get back across the river and back into the heart of Siam.

She forced herself to her feet and took a step. She felt a tugging at her heart, pulling her back to the river, but she couldn't stay here. Her eyes filled with tears once again, and she didn't fight them. She would not stop herself from grieving for Safi, the most gentle, loving, and intelligent creature she had ever met. She would never forget her friend, and she would never stop punishing herself for failing her vow to protect her.

For a long time, Kanita walked along the edge of the cliff, listening to the river below her. She didn't want to go back into the jungle and face the dangers it could present without Safi to help and protect her. But eventually, she didn't have a choice. The jungle encroached upon the cliff's edge and there was no way around it. She entered the jungle but walked slowly and carefully. She found a branch and used it as a walking stick, swinging it in front of her to scare away any snakes or spiders in her path. She was moving at a painfully slow rate compared to the large strides Safi had been able to take. She also had no way to cut through the brush. She didn't have a sword or even a knife to cut through the thick vines and leaves that blocked her path. She kept having to turn around and find another way. Even though she had her compass, she quickly discovered it was useless since she had to change directions so many times. She tried to generally head in a north-westerly direction, but she went back south and further east so many times, she was soon lost.

By the time darkness fell, she had no idea where she was in relation to the river and no idea which direction she should go once morning came. She found a large rock and leaned up against it to settle in for the night, wrapping one of her shawls around her. She was too nauseous to eat anything but was desperately thirsty. She couldn't remember the last time she had found fresh water. She realized that upon waking, her first goal needed to be survival. If she didn't find water soon, she would die. Only after that could she worry about getting back across the river.

***

She was awakened by the sensation of a million feathers tickling her leg. She opened her eyes and froze when she saw a large black centipede with dozens of feet crawling over her leg like a log. Even though she was terrified, she didn't move. She knew the bite of a centipede was poisonous, and many people said it was more painful than a cobra bite. She had no desire to find out if the claim was true or not, so she sat completely still. Eventually, the centipede completed its crawl over her leg and into some nearby mondo grass. Kanita jumped to her feet and ran as far away from the centipede as possible.

When she stopped, she took a deep breath. But the air did not smell of fresh morning dew. Smoke. Mixed with grilled meat. Someone was cooking nearby. She knew there was a possibility it was the rebel camp, but it could also be a village. Either way, there was sure to be water. She headed in the direction of the smells.

She started to hear the sounds of people walking around and men's voices. She crept along, low to the ground, trying to be as quiet as possible. She finally laid flat on her stomach and inched forward. To her dismay, it was indeed the rebel camp. There were a few tents scattered around, men who were well-armed, and several bamboo cages of animals such as wild cats, otters, and monkeys. She knew that many people made money by selling hides and live wild animals to the colonizers. Since Decha was a known rebel against the king, he was probably earning money for his cause by selling animals to the French.

She looked around and saw a large barrel next to one of the tents. There were several water skeins next to it, so it must be a rain barrel. Leaning next to it were several medium sized swords, perfect for hacking through the thick brush. She was surprised to see such things just lying around, but here in this remote place, the rebels must have thought no one would find them, much less dare to steal from them.

A tiny flutter of hope flitted through her belly. The rebels would never even know she was there. She could take some water skeins full of water and one of the swords and slip away easily.

She then wondered if it were possible for her to still save the prince. He must be tied up in one of the tents. She could use a sword to cut through the canvas, untie the prince, and they could slip into the jungle and disappear long before the rebels had any idea they were gone. If she saved the prince's life, the king might honor her. He could even give her some sort of reward. She could beg him to reinstate her father's position! She could go home!

Saving the prince wouldn't solve all of her problems—and it certainly wouldn't bring Safi back—but it was a good place to start. Kanita raised her head and licked her lips as she formulated a plan. She would need to be both quick and quiet, and she needed to figure out which tent held the prince—

The leaves covering her were moved aside as two men stepped in front of her. She looked up, her eyes wide. She'd been caught!

"Are you ever going to come out of there?" one of them asked her.

"We've been watching you for like twenty minutes," the other added.

"Uhh..." She tried to crawl away, but, of course, she was no match for the men. They grabbed her arms and dragged her into the camp as she screamed and kicked her feet.

The two men took her into a tent and then threw her to the floor at the feet of another man.

The man turned and looked at her. He was tall and broad and wore a huge sword on his back. He wasn't wearing a shirt, but his arms and chest were covered with tattoos. He wore loose pants but no shoes. He was smoking a long bamboo pipe she knew was popular with the Karen tribal people, but she couldn't tell if he was actually Karen.

"What brings you to my camp, little girl?" the man asked.

My camp. This had to be Decha. She sat up on her knees and looked around. There were probably half a dozen men in the tent. She had no chance of escape.

"Water," she whispered.

"What?" Decha asked, leaning down.

A Girl and Her Elephant

"I need water," she said again, her voice dry and cracked, and she realized her throat was still sore from screaming Safi's name. Her eyes watered at the thought, but she could not cry. Not now. She cleared her throat and tried to speak more clearly. "I need water. I haven't had anything to drink in days."

Decha stood back up and nodded to one of his men, who tossed him a water skein. He handed it to Kanita. She uncorked it and guzzled the water down, much of it escaping down the side of her face. She paused for breath, and then took another long swig.

"Slow down, girl," Decha said as he moved to a large chair in the middle of the room and sat down. "You'll make yourself sick."

Kanita stopped drinking and wiped her face with the back of her hand. "Thank you."

"Who are you?" he asked. "What are you doing here?"

"I'm lost," she admitted. She had no leverage with which to save herself. Her only hope was to try and talk her way out of this mess. "I only want to go home."

"And where is home?" he asked, leaning back and sucking on his pipe.

"Chiang Mai," she said.

Decha nodded. "Long way from here."

"I know," she said.

"Are you who I think you are?" Decha asked.

Kanita pondered this for a moment, and then slowly nodded her head. If he had heard of her, maybe she could use that to her advantage. "Yes," she admitted. "I'm the elephant girl."

Decha looked at his men, and then they all laughed.

"I can't believe we have the famous elephant girl in our midst!" he said, clapping his hands. "The girl who defied her father, ran away from a forced marriage, stole her *khong man*, and turned her bad omen elephant into a good luck one, spreading happiness through the villages of Siam!" The men all laughed again. "So where is this famous elephant?" Decha asked.

Kanita's head dropped to her chest. "She...she's gone," she said.

"Then how do I know it is really you?" Decha asked, sucking his pipe.

"You know I'm telling the truth," she said, looking him square in the eye.

Decha's lips curled into a smile. "Your husband, Chakri, is looking for you."

Her heart fell into her stomach. He was alive. And he was still searching for her.

"I...I don't know what you mean..." she stammered.

"Chakri is claiming his right as a husband over the girl with the elephant," Decha explained as he stood up. "He says he owns you since you kept the *khong man*. He is offering a handsome reward for your safe return."

Kanita started to panic. She stood up and backed away. "I'm not the elephant girl," she said.

"But I thought you were," Decha said, stepping toward her. "Were you lying then or are you lying to me now."

"I...I'm not...I have to get out..." She turned to run away even though she knew there was no hope for escape. Decha grabbed her and pulled down the back of her shirt. She screamed again. "Don't! Please!" she cried.

"Ah-ha!" Decha said, releasing her and letting her fall to the ground. "You are the elephant girl! You have the tattoo of a mahout family."

She crawled away from Decha toward the wall of the tent. Her tattoo! She had completely forgotten about it.

A Girl and Her Elephant

Since it was on her back where she couldn't see it, she often forgot it was even there. But Decha had known it would be there.

"Please," she begged. "Please don't give me back to Chakri! He's a bad man."

"Sorry, elephant girl," Decha said, nodding to his men. "But I need the money to wage my war against the king."

Two of the men grabbed her by the arms and dragged her away.

"No! Stop!" she yelled as she kicked her legs, but there was no way she could escape and nothing she could offer in exchange.

The men took her to another tent, one filled with more bamboo cages of wild animals. They took her to a large, empty cage, one probably used for tigers, and threw her inside before securing the cage with a chain. Then, they left the tent.

"Wait!" she called out. "You can't just leave me here!"

She grunted and kicked at the corner of her cage where the bamboo was secured with hemp rope.

"Hey," a groggy voice said. "Who...who's there?"

She gasped. She had completely forgotten about the prince, so she hadn't expected to hear another voice in the room.

"Prince Mongkut?" she asked.

"Yes, it is me," he said.

She then saw him in a cage across the room. As he came into focus, she gasped.

"Elephant girl?" he asked in disbelief.

"It's you!" she cried. It was the boy who had given her the compass.

CHAPTER FOURTEEN

"What are you doing here?" Mongkut asked, his face bright as he gripped the bars.

"Umm...rescuing you," Kanita said sheepishly.

Mongkut laughed. "Is this part of your plan? Distract Decha while the elephant storms the camp and breaks the cages?"

Kanita thought that would have been a good plan, but instead, she had to shake her head. "Safi's gone."

"Oh," Mongkut said, his excitement dropping but still holding onto a bit of hope. "I'm sorry to hear that. So, what was your plan? Why did you come here without her?"

"I don't know," Kanita said, sighing and leaning against the wall of her cage. "I only found the camp by accident. I thought I could sneak in and out without being seen, but they knew I was there as soon as I got close."

"Why did Decha capture you?" Mongkut asked. "What is your worth to him?"

"He said that Chakri, the man my father arranged for me to marry, is willing to pay a large price for my return,"

A Girl and Her Elephant

she said. "I guess he needs the money for his rebellion against the king."

Mongkut spit. "Decha is not a rebel, but a traitor. A terrorist!" he declared.

Kanita shrugged. "Whatever you say."

"It is not what *I* say," Mongkut said, lifting his chin with an arrogant pride. "It is what the king says."

Kanita looked at the prince and cocked her head. "The same king who sentenced an innocent baby elephant to death?"

Mongkut crossed his arms but did not reply.

"Sorry if I don't put much faith in anything that man has to declare," she said.

"That is heresy!" Mongkut growled, gripping the bars of his cage so tightly his knuckles were white. "Sedition! You could be put to death for such words."

Kanita looked away from the prince. Married to Chakri. Sent back to her abusive father. Sentenced to death by the king. All outcomes seemed equally bad to her at this point. At least death would be a quick end and she could start over again as a lower lifeform and begin her journey of atonement.

She had lost everything. Her beloved elephant. Her family. Her home. Her future. What did she have left? Her life, she supposed, but what was that worth without the rest of it?

"But if you help me get out of here," Mongkut continued. "I am sure I could be persuaded to convince my father to forget your evil words."

Kanita looked at him again and smiled. "Or if you die here, he'll never hear of them at all."

Mongkut pressed his lips into a thin line and his face went red. He shook the bamboo bars of his cage, but they barely moved. He turned away from her, and she chuckled. She had a feeling the prince was used to getting his way. And probably never had a girl dare to talk back to him before. But here in these cages, they were equals.

"Fine," he said, turning back to her once he got his anger under control. "If you can help me get out of here, I can speak to my father on your behalf and get you pardoned for everything."

Now Kanita was intrigued. "Everything?"

"Everything," he said. "He will reward you for saving me and can speak well of you to your parents."

"Can he reinstate my father as a mahout?" she asked, rising to her knees. If she could have her father's position restored, he might still take her back.

"The king can do whatever he wants," Mongkut said. "If that is the reward you ask for, the king could grant it."

Kanita licked her parched lips. Did she dare to hope? After everything that had happened, was there still a chance at redemption?

"And...your elephant," Mongkut said slyly.

"What about Safi?" Kanita asked, leaning closer to the cage bars.

"My father could pardon Safi," he said. "Even in death, he could forgive her of her crimes and have her enshrined in the Hall of Noble Beasts. She could be reincarnated as a higher being, or even be elevated to Heaven itself!"

She had been so distraught over losing Safi, she hadn't even considered what could happen to her in the next life. As a cursed, bad omen elephant, she would surely come back as a lesser being. But if the king, an emissary of the gods, pardoned her, spoke on her behalf, she could be saved from such a fate.

A Girl and Her Elephant

"He can do that?" Kanita asked. "Even though Safi is already dead?"

"Of course," he said. "We honor people and animals posthumously all the time."

"Okay!" she said, warmth blooming in her heart. "I'll do it! For my father and for Safi."

"Great!" Mongkut said. "So...how do we get out of here?"

Kanita looked around the cage. The door was secured with a chain, so there was no chance of her escaping that way. But the corners were tied together with hemp. They were knotted tightly, but they would at least be more vulnerable than the door. She crawled to one of the corners and started to kick at the joints.

"I already tried that," Mongkut said through gritted teeth.

"Just let me try, okay?" Kanita snapped back.

Mongkut growled in annoyance as Kanita continued kicking the corner of her cage. She realized it wasn't the best idea. These cages were designed to hold tigers and bears, strong animals with claws. If a tiger couldn't escape, what hope did she have? After a few minutes of no progress, she gave up and started looking for a new way out. She scanned the room, looking for a knife or anything sharp they could use to cut the rope.

"Do you see anything sharp?" she asked Mongkut.

"They aren't going to just leave weapons within reach," Mongkut argued.

Kanita sighed and did her best to keep from groaning. "One thing at a time," she explained patiently. "If you see something we could use to cut the ropes, *then* we will worry about how to reach it."

"I don't see—" Mongkut started to say, but he stopped

when the flap to the tent was pulled open and bright light streamed into the room.

Kanita blinked and shielded her eyes from the light. She couldn't see anything at first, but then she heard Decha's voice.

"She's right here, Chakri, my friend," he said.

Kanita's heart raced fast and she scooted to the back of the cage. The dark forms of the two men approached her cage, and one kneeled in front of the door. Her eyes cleared and she saw Chakri sitting only inches from her.

"We meet again, my beautiful Kanita," Chakri said.

Kanita couldn't help but let out a cry.

Chakri laughed. "I told you that you would be mine, pretty girl," he said. "One way or another."

"No!" Kanita yelled. "I'll never marry you! I'll never agree. I'd rather die."

Chakri stood up and kicked the cage. "That can be arranged!" he screamed at her.

The room went silent as Kanita, Decha, and the prince stared at Chakri. Kanita started to shake but did her best to keep her body under control. She couldn't let him know just how scared she was.

Chakri looked at Decha, who was frowning. He did not seem impressed by Chakri's threats against a girl in a cage.

Chakri cleared his throat and chuckled. "But I would never want harm to come to my sweet girl," he said. "She's been the object of my affection for many years. I am sure that once she sees how I will spoil her, she will come around."

Kanita knew that she could never accept Chakri as a husband, but she stayed quiet this time.

"Unfortunately," Decha said, patting Chakri on the

shoulder. "We are a simple people here in my camp. We have no honorable elder to oversee the union."

Chakri nodded. "I understand, my friend," he said. "But we have something better." He looked to the prince. "As someone ordained by Heaven, your other prisoner will surely be good enough to perform a simple marriage ceremony."

Decha laughed. "The boy is quite stubborn. But if you think you can get him to do as you ask..."

Chakri let out a chuckle from deep in his chest as he looked at the prince. He drew a long knife out and stuck it through the bamboo slats of the cage, pointing it at the prince.

"I'm sure he can be persuaded..." Chakri said.

Kanita's throat went dry as she watched Chakri threaten the prince. The man was insane! If the prince escaped or if Decha returned him to the king after receiving a ransom, he would certainly tell his father what happened. The king would have Chakri put to death for threating his child.

Decha slapped Chakri on the shoulder again. "I am sure the boy will comply," he said. "One way or another."

Mongkut spit on the ground. "Don't be so sure of that, traitor," he said to Decha.

Decha laughed. "You keep using that word," he said. "But I was not the one who sold my ancestral land to the foreign barbarians. I am only trying to preserve my country and my people. Your father is willing to give it away piece by piece to the highest bidder. Who is the real traitor to the people of Siam?"

Mongkut jumped forward and shook the bars of his cage. "Just let me out of here!" he screamed. "And I'll gut you like a fish!"

Decha and Chakri laughed at the prince's outburst and headed out of the tent.

"Get ready, sweet girl," Chakri said. "I'll be back soon." He then dropped the flap to the tent closed behind him.

Kanita's head dropped into her hands and she could not stop herself from wailing in despair.

"I just had an idea," Mongkut said, completely ignoring Kanita's distress. "If you marry Chakri, you'll be free! You can tell my father's men where Decha's camp is so they can come rescue me and kill Decha!"

"You idiot!" Kanita snapped. "I'll just be trading one jailer for another. I won't be free with Chakri. I'd be better off in this cage than married to that man."

"But if my father frees me," Mongkut said, "I can then send men after Chakri. I can have him arrested, even put to death if you wish. Then you'd be free too!"

"I'll be raped and dead by then," Kanita said.

"What?" Mongkut asked. "But...you'll be his wife. He said he loves you. You'll be fine in his care for just a little while until I can escape too."

Kanita shook her head as she thought about the way her father had hit her twice now, and how he regularly bullied her mother. True, he had never beaten her, at least not in front of her, but he terrorized her in his own way. And she knew plenty of other women in her village who were beaten by their husbands. It was considered just a part of married life. And most of those men were considered pillars of the community—village elders, mahouts, her father's friends and men he worked with. None of them were as dark and twisted as Chakri. As soon as they were married, he would insist on his "husbandly right." She would refuse, but he would take it by force. And if he didn't kill her, she would kill herself.

A Girl and Her Elephant

"Mongkut," Kanita said, her voice weak, tears forming in the corners of her eyes. "You can't depend on me to save you if you give me to Chakri. I won't even be able to save myself."

"Kanita," he said, determination in his voice. "It is better to be married than to be dead."

Kanita let out a small laugh. "You really know nothing about marriage."

"My father has over twenty wives and concubines," Mongkut said, his air of arrogance returning. "I will have twice that many one day."

"You have a lot to learn by then," Kanita said.

"We will get out of here alive," Mongkut said. "*Both* of us. And then you can teach me whatever you think I should know."

Kanita sighed. She had no hope now. Mongkut was a prince. He was used to getting his way and everything working out all right for him in the end. But Kanita knew better. She had learned the truth of life the hard way. She thought she had already lost everything, but she had been wrong. Instead of a quick death by the king's executioner, her death at Chakri's hands would be slow and painful.

But there was something to be said for Mongkut's conviction that they could still find a way out of this. She couldn't just lay down and die, she needed to keep going. She needed to keep fighting. To the very end.

"We might as well get this over with," she finally said.

CHAPTER FIFTEEN

Decha returned a few minutes later, his face in a scowl. He walked over to Kanita's cage and produced a key to open the lock. He removed the chains, opened the door, and offered Kanita his hand.

This surprised her. She had expected him to simply grab her and drag her out. She placed her hand in his and he gently pulled her to her feet.

"Are you going to run away?" he asked her.

She looked to the prince. If she did run away, she wouldn't get far. If she went through with the marriage, when she and Chakri left the camp, she might find one of the king's men and be able to alert him to Mongkut's location.

"No," she said truthfully. "I'm not going to run. I have nowhere to go."

Decha pressed his lips as though he was displeased by her answer, but he nodded and led her out of the tent. He took her back to the tent she had first met him in. She realized that this was Decha's personal tent, but it wasn't very personal. Not like the tent Mongkut had. It was dirty and disorganized. The items were quite random. Probably things he kept from the villages and military parties he raided.

"I want you to know, elephant girl," Decha said as he opened a trunk and rifled through it, "that this is nothing personal. I can understand your disdain for Chakri. He is an...odd man. If I could deny him the marriage, I would. But the deal is already struck. And he does have a prior claim—"

"This isn't your doing, Decha," Kanita interrupted. She thought it was strange that a man known for being a fierce rebel seemed to be in need of her consolation, but she gave it freely. This mess started long before he got involved, and most of her troubles were of her own doing. She could, at the very least, take responsibility for her own actions. "You didn't know what kind of man Chakri was when you accepted his money. And you have your own battles to fight. What's the life of one stupid girl who you'll never see again?"

She had meant her words to alleviate his guilt, but as he stood and walked over to her, his face looked even more grim.

"You remind me of my own daughter," he said.

"Did she have an elephant too?" she asked with a smile, trying to lighten the conversation.

He chuckled. "No. She loved monkeys. She could climb the trees with them and jump from one to another after them. She would give her mother and me a heart attack with her crazy antics."

Kanita laughed too. "It sounds like you love her very much."

Decha nodded and handed some silks to Kanita. "I do...I did...I always will."

Kanita took the silks and nodded, not asking more. She didn't know the details of what happened to Decha's daughter or wife, but she was certain their deaths must have had something to do with the loss of his home due to the king's dealings with the foreigners. She didn't blame him for his need to rebel—hadn't she also rebelled?—she was only sorry their paths had become entangled this way.

Decha motioned to a wicker screen in one corner of the room that she could change behind. For some reason, Decha had felt the need to give her new clothes for her wedding ceremony. The *sinh* skirt was a rich red silk with silver thread woven through the body of the garment. There was a simple silver wrap for her chest, and a long red *sabai* shawl to drape over her shoulder. There was also a thin silver band to wrap her hair in and two gold earrings.

She took the bag that still held the gold bracelets from her *khong man* and placed Mongkut's compass in with them. Then she secured the bag inside her waistband. Even though she should wear the *khong man* jewelry on her wedding day, she couldn't bear to look at them and what they represented.

She stepped out from behind the screen, and Decha motioned toward a small mirror sitting on a table. She nearly gasped when she saw herself. She looked like a proper bride. If she hadn't been marrying the worst man in the world, she would have almost felt proud of the woman she had become.

Decha stepped behind her and fastened a gold necklace around her neck. Then, he turned her to face him.

"As long as you and Chakri are in my camp," he said, "I will make sure he treats you honorably."

She nodded and looked down. Her hands trembled as her fingers touched the necklace at her throat. She didn't

A Girl and Her Elephant 121

want to cry, but the enormity of the situation was settling on her shoulders. She was scared. Decha might be able to protect her for a few minutes, but once Chakri had her alone and she was his wife, no one—not even the king—could protect her from him. She would be his property and he could do with her what he willed.

But she would have to survive. If she could live just long enough to see the prince rescued, Mongkut would honor his promise to see her father restored to his position and Safi pardoned. She might still come to a sad end in this life, but in the next one, maybe she wouldn't come back as a beetle.

"Come," Decha said, moving toward the tent's opening and pulling back the flap. There was no point in delaying what was about to happen.

As she stepped out of the tent, all of Decha's men had gathered for the ceremony, which was being held in the middle of the camp. The men clapped and some were playing long drums. It appeared that Decha was doing his best to make this seem like a happy occasion.

The ceremony was missing most of the key elements—there were no monks, no gated approach for the groom, and, of course, her parents were absent—but whatever aspects of a proper ceremony Decha could provide, he did.

As Decha led Kanita through the crowd, several of his men released some of the monkeys and birds they had captured to honor Kanita's ancestors.

The crowd parted and there standing before Kanita were Chakri and Mongkut. Kanita's heart froze when she saw Chakri standing before her, a wide smile on his face. She instinctually squeezed Decha's hand, and he squeezed back. She looked up at Decha, and he gave her a reassuring smile. She willed herself to calm down and looked back at Chakri.

Chakri was wearing a *ratcha pataen* outfit—a white Nehru-style jacket and red *chong kraben* pants. But his fine clothes did not distract from the leering look in his eyes or the sneer on his lips. She nearly wanted to vomit when Decha placed her hand in Chakri's.

Together, Kanita and Chakri faced Prince Mongkut. Mongkut was also wearing clean clothes, but his hands and feet were in chains, and two of Decha's strongest men flanked the prince on either side. It was a stark reminder that, in spite of Decha's heartfelt words toward her, she and Mongkut were still prisoners.

Kanita and Chakri kneeled on two pillows before Mongkut and folded their hands in front of them. She sighed in relief to be free of Chakri's grasp, if only for a moment.

Mongkut placed a *mong kul*, two crowns woven from a single piece of string and still tied together, on Kanita's and Chakri's heads, symbolizing that they would be joined together for the rest of their lives.

As the crown touched Kanita's head, she could not stifle a cry from escaping her throat. *Forever*. She was to be tied to Chakri for the rest of her life. As much as she wanted to still find a way to save Mongkut, she hoped the rest of her life would be short.

"Stop crying," Chakri hissed at her.

She pressed her hands to her chest and sniffled, doing her best to calm down, but she couldn't quite stop the tears.

Decha then handed a shell filled with water to Mongkut, which Mongkut held aloft.

"I pray that Heaven will bless this union," Mongkut said.

"May the birds in the sky, the fish in the sea, the beasts of the forest—"

A loud trumpeting disrupted the ceremony and the ground shook violently. Everyone looked around in a panic.

Everyone except Kanita.

"Safi!" Kanita yelled.

The men screamed and scattered as Safi charged through the camp, trumpeting so loud the leaves that shaded the ceremony fell from the trees.

Kanita stood and ran toward Safi, her heart full to bursting. She felt the *mong kul* fall from her head, but she didn't look back. She heard Chakri yell at her, but she didn't stop running. She forgot about Mongkut. All she knew was that Safi was alive!

"Safi!" Kanita cried again as she ran toward her elephant and jumped into the safe embrace of Safi's trunk. They hugged each other and Kanita let the tears fall, this time from joy. Safi then lifted Kanita to her back and turned to leave the camp.

Only now did Kanita allow herself a glance back. She saw Decha issuing orders, Chakri screaming, and Mongkut standing in shock. For a moment, she thought they should go back for Mongkut, but then she remembered that he was still in chains. They wouldn't be able to free him. She made a promise to herself that they would find the king's men as soon as possible and send help for Mongkut.

Kanita looked back ahead at the trail Safi had already blazed for them. The camp was small, so they would be back in the jungle in only a moment. She had no idea what they would do then, but it didn't matter! Safi was alive! Anything was possible!

Then, Safi stumbled. She trumpeted and groaned as her massive body started to crash to the ground and she couldn't stop herself. Kanita jumped away as far as she could to keep herself from being crushed. She hit the ground and rolled, then slammed hard into a tree.

Her head was spinning. She tried to sit up, but she fell back down. She rolled to her side and opened her eyes.

"Safi?" she moaned. Decha's men must have sprung into action after their initial shock wore off. They had managed to run a long rope in Safi's path and then held it taught enough to cause her to trip. The men quickly hammered metal pins into the ground and tied the ropes to them to pin Safi down to the ground.

Safi trumpeted and struggled, but the men—poachers that they were—knew how to capture an elephant.

Kanita got to her knees and crawled toward Safi, calling her name. "Safi! I'm here!"

Safi groaned and cried. She reached her trunk out toward Kanita.

"Give me that gun!" Chakri yelled.

Kanita looked over and saw Chakri stomping toward Safi with a rifle. Kanita shouldn't have been surprised to see one in a poacher's camp. She scrambled to her feet and ran toward Chakri, grabbing the barrel of the gun with both hands.

"No!" she screamed. "I won't let you!"

Chakri tried to shake her off, but her grip was too strong. He'd have to kill her to get her to let go.

"One way or another," Chakri yelled at her, "I'm going to kill that elephant!"

"That's enough!" Decha yelled. "Give me the gun, Chakri!"

Chakri looked at Decha and could see the man was serious.

"Fine," Chakri said, handing Decha the gun with Kanita still gripping the barrels. "You do it."

"Decha, no!" Kanita yelled, not loosening her grip.

"I'm not going to kill the elephant," Decha said. "You have my word, Kanita."

"Kanita is my wife," Chakri yelled. "Her property now belongs to me. That is my elephant and I want it dead!"

Decha pressed his lips and looked from Chakri, to Kanita, to Safi. "Safi can stay here," Decha said.

"She won't," Kanita said. "She survived falling into the river and being swept downstream. Somehow, she found her way back to me. She will never leave my side."

Decha sighed and shook his head, unsure of what to do. Kanita didn't know either. Once she and Chakri left the camp, she wouldn't even be able to protect herself from Chakri, much less Safi.

"If you kill Safi," Kanita said to Chakri, "I'll kill myself. But—" she said, stopping him from interrupting. "If you promise to spare Safi's life, I...I will marry you. Willingly. And I will never give you trouble again."

"Done," Chakri said without a second of hesitation. "You heard the girl, Decha. Let's complete the ceremony."

CHAPTER SIXTEEN

Once again, Kanita was kneeling before the prince with her hands folded in front of her for the wedding ceremony with Chakri.

"Nice of you to just run off like that," Mongkut mumbled to Kanita as Decha went to refill the ceremonial shell with water.

"We would have come back for you," she whispered.

"Shut up, both of you," Chakri barked at them.

Kanita looked over her shoulder back at Safi, who was still tied up. Chakri insisted that Safi stay subdued until they left the camp. He didn't trust her not to rampage again. Her and Safi's eyes met and Kanita nodded in reassurance. She may have promised not to run away again, but together, they would still find some way out of this mess. As small and unreasonable as it might be, she once again had hope.

She had Safi.

Decha returned with the shell of water and handed it to Mongkut. Decha's lips were pressed in a thin line. Mongkut's hands shook slightly as he took the shell and looked to Kanita as if for permission to continue. She gave him a small nod. She glanced around at the rest of Decha's men. They were no longer pretending this was a celebration but stood around solemnly. This was the only wedding Kanita had been to where every person in attendance was miserable. Even Chakri did not seem happy to finally be getting what he wanted. His face was flushed and he kept urging Mongkut to hurry.

Mongkut raised the shell and repeated his blessing from earlier. "I pray that Heaven will bless this union. May the birds in the sky, the fish in the sea, the beasts of the forest..." He paused and looked at Safi, who squirmed and grunted under her bounds.

"Get on with it," Chakri grumbled.

Mongkut cleared his throat. "May the birds in the sky, the fish in the sea, the beasts of the forest bless you." He then poured half of the water out on Kanita's folded hands, then he poured out the other half on Chakri's.

Kanita's heart beat fast in her chest. She had done the one thing she swore she would never do. The thing that had caused her to run away in the first place. She had lost everything and still ended up married to Chakri. Well, she hadn't lost everything. She had Safi back, and that was all that mattered. She only hoped that Chakri would keep his end of the bargain and not try to harm Safi once they left Decha's camp.

The prince then stepped forward and tied a white thread around Kanita's wrist, then he did the same for Chakri, to wish them happiness. Decha stepped forward and did the same. Kanita and Chakri would be expected to wear the strings for three days. Kanita could barely imagine what her life would be like three days from now.

"You may rise," the prince said, his voice nearly cracking. "As husband...and wife."

Chakri eagerly gripped Kanita's hand and wrapped his arm around her shoulder, holding her closely to him as they turned to face Decha's men, who clapped halfheartedly, if they clapped at all. Safi whimpered, but had grown tired of struggling beneath the ropes.

"And now, my little woman," Chakri said, turning Kanita to face him. He leaned in to kiss her, but Kanita turned her head, forcing him to kiss her cheek, her jaw, and then her neck, which might have been worse than had he only kissed her on the lips.

Chakri laughed as she struggled in his arms. "My new bride is quite feisty!" he said, but none of the other men laughed with him. "I like that in a girl. Come, wife." He tugged on her arm as he walked away from Decha through the crowd. "I hope, Decha, my friend, that you don't mind if I use your tent to...complete the marriage."

Kanita's knees nearly collapsed beneath her and she felt the bile rise in her throat. This was what she had been dreading most of all.

"No!" Decha said with enough force that he seemed to even startle himself.

Chakri froze and shot Decha an angry look. "What?" he asked.

"I mean..." Decha cleared his throat and then smiled. "This is your wife, not a common whore. You need a proper bedding ceremony. I don't have a gold tray or any of the auspicious items to bless your union. And her mother is not here to turn down the blanket..."

"Bah!" Chakri sneered. "All superstitious nonsense. I've waited a long time for this, Decha—"

"Then what is a few days more?" Decha interrupted. "Her village is near yours. You can ride back home with your wife atop a white elephant and then have her parents bless your union as is only proper. Sounds better than bedding her here in my filthy camp full of rowdy men." Decha then looked around at his men, who laughed in agreement.

"This is ridiculous," Chakri said.

"Not to me!" Kanita chimed in. "This is my wedding. Everything should be done the right way."

Chakri shook her arm. "You'll speak with I allow it!" he snapped.

"Now, now," Decha said, patting Chakri on the back and pulling him away from Kanita. "Have a drink, my friend! Let's celebrate!"

The other men cheered and followed Decha and Chakri to the center of camp, where they built a large bonfire.

"Good thing you have Decha looking out for you," Mongkut said as he stepped up behind her.

Kanita turned to him and saw that he was still bound and two of Decha's men were accompanying him.

"For now," Kanita said. "But once we leave the camp..."

"You'll be fine," the prince said, far surer of his words than Kanita felt. "You will have your elephant with you. And you are pretty clever. I'm sure you will find a way out of this mess. Just...don't forget your friends." He said the last part as nearly a whisper so his guards wouldn't hear.

Kanita nodded. She couldn't forget that part of the reason she had gone through with the marriage was to find help to rescue Mongkut, which would mean betraying Decha—the man who just saved her from Chakri. She felt a twisting in her gut. She couldn't abandon Mongkut, but if the king's men found Decha, they would surely kill him.

One of the men pushed Mongkut forward, and they walked back to the tent with the cages. Kanita sighed and looked around the camp. The bonfire was very large now, and the men were roasting some chickens over it. They were all drinking heavily. She could see Chakri swaying back and forth as he spoke to Decha with his arms waving. Decha was drinking as well, but he didn't appear drunk. He only smiled as Chakri continued yelling something she couldn't hear.

Kanita walked across the camp to Safi's side. Safi grunted and tried to stand up again, but she couldn't.

"Shh," Kanita cooed. "We will leave soon. Probably first thing tomorrow. Chakri will not want to delay our stay here any longer than he has to."

Safi let out a huff.

Kanita nodded. "I know. It's dreadful. But we have to be patient." She leaned down and kissed Safi's cheek. "You are alive! We are together. That is most important. Everything else will follow, I'm sure of it." In truth, she wasn't sure of anything, but she shoved her own fears and doubts aside to comfort her friend.

Safi sighed and relaxed a bit. Kanita kissed Safi again and patted her nose before standing up. From across the camp, Chakri was still yelling at Decha, now loudly enough for her to hear.

"I have paid and paid, and still I do not have my bride!" he shouted, and Kanita's face went hot. Even drunk, if he was enraged enough, he could still force her to his bed.

"I paid the *khong man*," Chakri went on. "I paid her parents the dowry. I paid *you* a ransom. And I still don't have my girl."

"You'll have the girl—" Decha tried to say, but Chakri continued his rampage.

"On your terms!" Chakri said. "On your day. In your way. Where...where is she?"

Chakri looked around, and Kanita dropped low to the

A Girl and Her Elephant

ground, hoping he wouldn't see her in his drunken state. He wobbled and squinted his eyes, but it seemed he couldn't see clearly.

Decha waved a couple of his men over. "Take him to my tent," he said. "The bed is waiting for you."

"That's more like it!" Chakri said as he relied on the men to help him walk.

Once he was gone, Decha caught sight of Kanita and waved her over to him. She hesitated, but then approached.

"He'll be angry when he realizes I'm not there," she said, her arms crossed.

"He is so drunk, I'm sure he will pass right out once he sits down," he said confidently.

Kanita nodded. "Thank you."

Decha gave her a small smile and handed her a cup of drink. He then motioned to a log next to the fire for them to sit on. "It was the least I could do," he said.

"I still appreciate it," Kanita said, sipping at the strong alcohol in her cup.

"If there is anything else I can do," Decha said, "you have only to name it."

"You could release Mongkut," she said without hesitating.

Decha looked at her, his eyes wide with surprise. Then he chuckled and looked away from her, back at the fire. "You are a brave girl, Kanita. Never doubt that."

Kanita looked to the fire as well, the flames seeming to glow brighter as the sun set. "But you aren't going to release him?" she asked.

"You know I cannot," Decha said. "You see how few men I have. How we live in this remote place. I may have a fearsome reputation, but I am losing this battle. Mongkut is the only card against the king I have left to play."

"But if you kill him," Kanita said, "the king will never stop pursuing you. You'll lose and you'll have the prince's blood on your hands."

"I will not harm the prince," Decha said. "You have no need to worry about that. I will only use him to force the king to give me back my kingdom."

"Your...your kingdom?" Kanita asked. "You're a king too?"

Decha laughed. "You really have no idea who I am, do you?"

Kanita shook her head. "I've heard my father talk about the British and the French, but he is loyal to the king, so I never heard a bad word against him."

"I am the king of the Kingdom of Vientiane," Decha said. "Or I was, until the king of Siam betrayed me. He agreed to a treaty with the French that absorbed my country into Laos, which is under French control. Overnight, we went from being a separate nation into being French vassals. Slaves!"

"I'm sorry," Kanita said, though she doubted Decha's account was so simple. The king probably had his own version of events, not that she would ever get to hear the king's side.

"All I want is my country back," Decha said. "Mongkut is the key to that."

Kanita sighed. She now knew that there was no way she was going to be able to convince Decha to release Mongkut. Either he would have to release Mongkut on his own in exchange for the return of his country—which she doubted the king could do if his country were now under the control of the French—or she would have to reveal the location of the camp to the king's men. She felt sick at the thought of betraying Decha, but she knew that she wasn't going to have a choice.

"The least you could do is treat him better," she said, trying to lighten the mood. "I'm sure he would enjoy a drink as well."

"I cannot risk his escape," Decha said.

Kanita motioned to the darkness of the jungle. "Where is he going to go?"

Decha sighed. "Fine." He waved one of his men over. "Bring me the prince." The man nodded and ran off. Decha and Kanita laughed as they took a drink together.

"Decha!" the man shouted as he came back. "The prince is gone!"

"What?" Decha roared as he jumped to his feet. "How?"

"Idiot," Kanita mumbled under her breath. The prince wouldn't survive a minute on his own in the jungle at night!

"I don't know," the man said. "The guards are dead and the cage unlocked!"

"Dead?" Decha asked. "How is that possible?"

"Chakri!" Kanita said. "Where is Chakri?"

She and Decha looked at each other and then ran for Decha's tent. Just as Kanita expected, Chakri was gone.

"He must have kidnapped the prince and ran into the jungle," Kanita said. "He's going to ransom the prince himself."

"They will be dead by morning," Decha grumbled, and Kanita knew he was right.

CHAPTER SEVENTEEN

"We have to go after them," Kanita said.

"Are you crazy?" Decha asked. "It's too dangerous, even for me. How *you* survived is a miracle."

"I have an elephant," Kanita said. "Safi and I can find him. Elephants have keen senses. It's how she found her way back to me. Chakri and the prince can't have gotten far."

"No," Decha said. "I won't risk it. If Chakri is really gone, then at first light, you can go home. That's one small thing I can do right in all this mess."

"Really?" Kanita asked. "You'll set me free?"

"I have no reason to keep you prisoner now," he said. She realized that he already had Chakri's money, so if Chakri left her behind, Decha had no reason to make her stay. If anything, she would only be a drain on their limited resources.

She could leave. Forget Chakri. Forget everything and go home and beg her parents for forgiveness. They could start over.

But she couldn't leave Mongkut. She thought back to the

beginning of her journey, how she had been filthy, lost, and hungry. Mongkut had helped her. And here at the camp, Mongkut had been her friend. They had a plan to escape together. She couldn't abandon him now.

Decha had been giving his men orders, having them search the camp to make sure Chakri wasn't simply hiding somewhere.

"Decha!" Kanita said. "I can do it! Let me go find Mongkut."

"No!" Decha said firmly. "Go to my tent where you will be safe and stay there until morning."

"But—" she tried one more time.

"Now!" he ordered.

Kanita pouted and held her tongue. No amount of arguing was going to change his mind. Even though she was a married woman now—thanks to him—who had survived in the jungle for weeks on her own, he still saw her as a helpless little girl. Well, she would show him.

She went to his tent, as ordered, but she wouldn't stay there. It didn't take long for her to find what she was looking for—a large knife. She poked her head back out of the tent. Everyone was busy, rushing around, not paying her any attention. She ran over to Safi and used the knife to quickly cut the elephant loose.

Safi trumpeted as she stood, grateful to be able to stretch her legs. Kanita grabbed Safi's ear and swung up onto her back as the elephant rose up off the ground.

"Let's go!" Kanita said. "Let's find Mongkut!"

Safi turned and ran out of the camp and into the jungle. She didn't need to be told which direction to go. Her elephant senses would lead her straight to the prince—and to Chakri.

The men in the camp yelled and waved their arms to get

Safi and Kanita to stop, but Kanita paid them no mind. She did look back for Decha, though. Their eyes met briefly, and she smirked. He smiled and shook his head, but he made no move to stop her. They gave each other a respectful nod before Kanita turned back to the jungle and prepared herself for what she and Safi might face ahead.

The jungle was dark, but the moon was still bright. Kanita kept her head down until her eyes adjusted to keep from being knocked off of Safi's back by a branch or vine. They didn't have to go far before she started hearing the sounds of a struggle.

Kanita and Safi came to a break in the trees and saw Chakri and Mongkut struggling.

"Come on, you little brat," Chakri said. "I'm taking you home!"

"Let go of me!" Mongkut yelled. "You're a monster! I won't let my father think you are some sort of hero."

Chakri then did the unthinkable and punched Mongkut in the face. Kanita gasped as Mongkut fell to the ground. Chakri had just struck the son of the king! The crown prince! If the king found out, he'd have Chakri killed.

Chakri seemed to slowly realize what he had done. He started kicking the prince. "You'll not be the ruin of me!" he screamed.

Kanita slid down off of Safi and ran to the prince. "Stop!" she yelled, pushing Chakri away and pulling out her knife.

"You!" Chakri said, grabbing her arm and shaking her, causing her to drop the knife. "This is all your fault! If you'd just agreed to the marriage in the first place—"

Kanita spit in his face. "I'd never marry you willingly!"

Chakri slapped her cheek.

Safi trumpeted and stomped forward. She swung her

trunk at Chakri, but Chakri ducked. He pushed Kanita away and grabbed the prince, dragging him to his feet. He then grabbed the knife Kanita had dropped and held it to the prince's throat.

"Say back, you dumb beast!" Chakri yelled. "Or I'll kill your precious prince!"

Safi stopped, but let out a loud trumpet in protest.

Kanita felt the ground around her until she found a rock. She stood up and threw it at Chakri, hitting him in the side of the head.

Chakri grunted and stumbled to the side. Mongkut turned to try and escape Chakri's grasp, but Chakri was too strong.

"Let him go!" Kanita yelled. "I'm the one you want!"

Chakri growled and tossed Mongkut to the side, seeming to forget about Safi for a moment. His mind still clouded by the alcohol.

Safi stepped forward and swung at Chakri again, but he ran beyond her reach behind a tree. Safi started to go after him but stopped when she heard Mongkut call for help.

"Kanita!" Mongkut yelled. "I'm stuck! Hurry!" Kanita ran toward Mongkut, but when she got close, he yelled for her to stop. "Look out! Quicksand!"

Kanita froze in her tracks just beyond the edge of the sandy pit. Mongkut had already sunk nearly to his knees.

"Stay calm!" she said. "Lift one foot, then the other. Slowly!"

But Mongkut was already in a panic. He tried to pull his feet loose too quickly, which only made him sink faster. "I can't! Hurry! Do something!"

"Okay, okay!" she said, waving Safi over. "Safi, try to reach him and pull him out."

Safi snuffled and moved to the edge of the pit. She

reached out with her trunk and was barely able to reach Mongkut's hand.

"Lean forward!" Kanita yelled. Mongkut strained to reach a little further while Safi stepped dangerously close to the edge of the quicksand. "You've almost got him!" Kanita said.

"You're mine!" Chakri yelled as he grabbed Kanita from behind and dragged her away from the quicksand and back into the jungle.

Safi trumpeted and started to follow after them, but Kanita stopped her.

"No!" Kanita yelled. "Save Mongkut!"

Safi grunted and hesitated, but then she turned back to Mongkut.

Kanita was on her own, but she wasn't alone. She just had to survive for a few minutes. As soon as Safi freed Mongkut, she would come for her. She knew it!

Kanita stopped suddenly, forcing Chakri to stumble. But as he fell, he grabbed Kanita's ankle, causing her to trip forward as well. As she hit the ground, she rolled forward. She was tumbling down a ridge, and she could hear Chakri rolling after her.

When she hit the ground, she stood up quickly so she could run, but Chakri was too fast. He was right behind her. He grabbed her and forced her to the ground. He gripped her wrists and straddled her waist.

"Now, no one will come between us," he said. "You will be mine!"

"I'll...never...submit..." she said as she felt him pin her arms to the ground.

Chakri leaned in and licked her cheek.

She groaned as she looked around for anything that she could use as a weapon. Anything that might help her escape.

That was when she realized they were in a clearing very similar to one she had been in before. Besides Chakri's grunts, she couldn't hear any other sounds of the jungle.

But then she heard one. The low growl of a cobra.

"Chakri!" she whimpered. "We...we have to go...It's not safe!"

"Shut up!" he yelled. "No more excuses!"

Her eyes darted around as she looked for the snake she knew was here. Then, she heard the hissing growl again, and it was coming from above her! She looked over Chakri's shoulder and saw the massive black snake hovering over him, its fangs bared.

"Chakri..." she started to say, but he released one of her wrists and slapped her across the face again.

The quick movement startled the snake, and it lunged, locking its fangs into Chakri's shoulder.

Chakri lifted up off of Kanita and let out a horrified scream. Kanita scooted out from under him and watched in terror as the snake reared back and then bit Chakri again, this time on his leg. Chakri swung his fist at the snake, but the snake was quick and strong. The snake coiled itself around Chakri's torso and latched onto his neck. This time, the snake would not let go.

Kanita pulled her eyes away and ran out of the cobra's den. She knew there was nothing she could do. There was no cure for the bite of a cobra.

Panting for each breath, Kanita ran back to the quicksand pit just as Safi pulled Mongkut safely back onto solid ground. Mongkut collapsed in exhaustion.

"Safi!" Kanita cried, wrapping her arms around her friend's trunk. "You did it! You saved him!"

Safi held her tightly, and Kanita knew that Safi would hold her forever if she could.

"It's okay," Kanita said, patting Safi's trunk. "Everything is okay now. We are all safe."

"Ch-Chakri?" Mongkut coughed.

Kanita let go of Safi and kneeled by Mongkut's side. She used her *sabai* to wipe the sand from his face. "He's gone," she said. "Dead."

"Did...did you...?" He couldn't quite form the question.

She shook her head. "We fell into a cobra den. I tried to warn him—"

Mongkut squeezed her hand. "I believe you," he said.

She considered insisting that it was true, that she hadn't killed Chakri with her own hands. But as the prince laid down, nearly passing out from exhaustion, she supposed it didn't matter. Chakri was dead, and he could never hurt her again.

She leaned back against Safi's leg, feeling worn out herself now that she could relax for a moment. Safi gently placed her trunk on Kanita's shoulder, and the three of them fell asleep.

CHAPTER EIGHTEEN

Thankfully, they didn't sleep long. After only a couple of hours, Safi woke up and started shuffling her feet anxiously, which woke Kanita. Kanita leaned over and shook Mongkut awake.

"Huh? What?" Mongkut groaned.

"We have to go," Kanita said.

"But it's still dark," Mongkut said.

"I know," Kanita said. "That's why we need to go. Decha will come looking for us at first light, I'm sure of it. We need to get as far away from here as possible."

"Good idea," Mongkut said as he forced himself to stand. "How are we going to...oh." He looked nervous as Kanita easily climbed up on Safi's back.

"Haven't you ever ridden an elephant before?" Kanita asked.

"Not without a basket, and steps to climb up and down," he said.

Kanita laughed and held her hand down to him. He grabbed it and scrambled up onto Safi's back behind her.

"I'll be sure to tell Safi to go slow for you," Kanita said with a smirk.

"Let's just go," he sighed, rolling his eyes.

"Where are we going?" Kanita asked as Safi started walking.

"Bangkok," Mongkut said. "I need to go home."

Kanita gulped, feeling nervous about heading toward the king, but she knew it was what they had to do. She pulled the prince's compass out of her bag to see what direction they were heading in. She wasn't surprised to see they were already heading south.

"Safi has known the right way to go all along," Kanita said as she patted Safi's head.

They rode in silence for a few minutes, but finally, Mongkut spoke again.

"I will tell my father what happened," he said. "I will ask him to pardon Safi and to reinstate your father's position, but I cannot promise you that he will listen to me."

Kanita felt tears sting her eyes. "I know," she said. "I hope the king will be grateful enough for your return that he will spare Safi's life, but I know you cannot force him to do the right thing."

"If you wish," Mongkut said, "you can just take me as far as the nearest village. As soon as I find my father's men, they will escort me home safely. Then you could go wherever you want."

It was a tempting offer. She and Safi could just leave once again. They could head into Annam, or even go back to Decha and help him fight for his cause. She was sure he could use an elephant in his battle against the king.

"No," she finally said. "I will go with you to see the king. We cannot keep living on the run. It is time to face whatever consequences are waiting for us."

"Chakri is dead," Mongkut said. "Can't you just go home?"

She shook her head. "My father was disgraced and lost his position. Elephants are expensive to keep. No one will believe that Chakri did not...take me as a proper wife. I have no money, save for what is left of my *khong man*, but that won't last long. It will be very difficult for me to ever find a husband, if I want one at all. And I don't know how my mother and I would be able to earn enough money to support the three of us, much less Safi as well. No, I cannot go home as I am—disgraced and Safi still cursed. Either the king pardons us or we will not be able to go home at all."

"I admire your determination," Mongkut said. "Can I borrow some?"

"For what?" she asked.

"For when I speak to my father," he said.

"About me and Safi?" she asked.

"No," he said. "That will be easy. You saved my life. I owe you a great debt I can never pay. No, I need your strength to speak to my father about Decha and the foreign treaties."

"What do you mean?" Kanita asked.

"I heard some of what he told you, about losing his kingdom," he said. "You might not have known who Decha was, but I did. He has been a thorn in my father's side for years. The situation is not as simple as Decha explained it to you, but he's not wrong either."

The conversation lulled as Safi crested a hill and they watched the sunrise over the jungle below them.

"He saved my life," Kanita finally said. "If Chakri had gotten his way, he might have killed me. If he hadn't, I'm not sure I would have been able to live with myself."

"There's that too," Mongkut said. "He showed himself to be an honorable man in protecting you. I don't know what

I'll be able to do for him, if anything, but I hope I have the courage to try. These foreign treaties...something must change."

"If anyone can bring forth the changes needed to make a stronger Siam," Kanita said, "I'm sure it's you."

The rest of the journey to Bangkok was mostly quiet and uneventful. They avoided the towns and villages, but Mongkut was able to use Kanita's *khong man* to buy them food and other supplies they needed for the journey. But when they finally arrived at the capital city, they could hide no longer.

At the edge of town, Mongkut reveled himself to the king's guards. Initially, the guards tried to arrest Kanita and take Safi into custody, but Mongkut ordered the guards to instead escort Kanita and Safi with him to the palace.

Kanita had never been to Bangkok, or any large city, before. She was awed by the sheer size of it and the number of people she saw. She was sure her whole village would fit in one small neighborhood in the sprawling capital. Once inside the city, she could no longer even see the jungle. She felt as though she were in a different world.

As they walked through the city, people began to crowd around and follow them.

"Bless you, prince!" someone finally yelled, then many of the people started yelling at the prince, both blessings and asking for blessings in return.

"It's the good luck elephant!" Kanita heard someone else say. At that, the crowds began to push in close as the people tried to touch Safi, hoping a bit of luck might be transferred to them. The guards had to stay vigilant to keep the crowds back so no one would accidentally fall under Safi's lumbering feet. Kanita was shocked that rumors about Safi had traveled so far, and that people in the city would believe in such things. But if the people believed that Safi was good luck and not bad luck, maybe the king would believe it too. Kanita waved to the people, and Safi made happy trumpets at them, which always led to cheers.

They finally reached the bridge that led to Rattanakosin Island, where the Grand Palace was located. The palace walls and buildings were a bright white, like a perfect pearl. The palace roofs were a gleaming red, and golden spires upon the various watts situated throughout the palace grounds shined like the sun. Kanita had never seen anything like it, even in her dreams.

As they approached the throne hall, Kanita and Mongkut slid down from Safi's back. Kanita was wondering if Safi would be allowed to climb the steps and enter the building when the doors opened and the king himself came out to meet them.

"Get down," Mongkut whispered to Kanita.

"What?" she asked, but Mongkut had already dropped to his knees and bowed his head to his father. Kanita looked around and saw that everyone else had not just dropped to their knees, but were performing a full kowtow with their foreheads to the ground and their hands folded in front of them. Kanita followed their example and kowtowed as well.

"My son!" the king said. "We are so glad you have returned to us safely!" The king drew Mongkut to his feet and squeezed his arms tightly, though he did not quite hug him. "Your mother has been beside herself with worry." He motioned to a woman next to him, who did not restrain herself from embracing and kissing her son.

"I am happy to be home," Mongkut said. "But I would not be here now if not for Kanita and her elephant, Safi."

The king grimaced. "Is this not the bad omen elephant I ordered destroyed many years ago?"

Kanita felt her cheeks go hot with anger at the king's words, but she bit her tongue. She would give Mongkut his chance to speak for her as promised.

"Yes," Mongkut said. "But she is not a bad omen elephant, she is a hero. She saved my life."

The king looked up at Safi, who cocked her head to the side and looked back at the king. The king then looked down at Kanita.

"Stand up, girl," he ordered.

Kanita did as she was told, but kept her eyes averted.

"You are the daughter of my *former* lead mahout?" he asked.

"I am," she said.

"You are aware that I removed him from his position for betraying me?" the king asked.

"Yes, Your Majesty," she said.

"And that this was already a kindness on my part?" he continued. "I was well within my right to put him to death."

Kanita shook with fear at the king's words. She had never considered that the king could have killed her father.

"The king is merciful," she said, her words coming out strangled.

The king turned back to Mongkut. "Did you know this same elephant attacked the mahout, the girl's father? His leg was badly mangled. He cannot walk."

Kanita gasped and forced her hand to her mouth. Safi had injured her father badly! The king would say that Safi was dangerous and put her to death! It would all be for nothing!

"It...it was an accident," Mongkut said. "The elephant was only protecting Kanita, I'm sure of it."

Kanita fell back to the ground at the feet of the king. "Please, blame me! Punish me! I ran away from home! I dishonored my father! I stole the *khong man*! Spare Safi. She is innocent! She would never harm another living thing except in the protection of me. Please, kill me. Not Safi!"

The king seemed shocked by her outburst. He opened and closed his mouth several times while he decided on a response.

"K-kill you?" he finally asked. "You would die for your elephant?"

"She would do the same for me," Kanita said. "She nearly did."

Safi stepped forward and laid her trunk on Kanita's back in comfort and snuffled.

The king shook his head as he tried to make sense of the scene.

"It is true, father," Mongkut finally added. "Safi nearly died. And she could have left Kanita. Gone to live in the jungle, find other elephants, but she came back to Decha's camp and saved Kanita, and she saved me as well."

The king paced as he considered Mongkut's and Kanita's words. He finally stopped and nodded.

"Such loyalty, even in an animal, should be rewarded," he said. Then he reached down and took Kanita's hands in his own and drew her to her feet. "I owe you a great debt, you and your elephant, for saving my son. Whatever you want, you have only to name it, and it is yours."

"Pardon Safi," she said, and Safi trumpeted.

"It is done," the king said. "Anything else? Riches, titles, land. What will you have of me?"

"My father," Kanita said. "Can you name him a royal mahout again?"

The king's face went grim. "I am sorry, Kanita," he said. "But with his injuries, I fear he will never be able to train elephants again. However, I will grant him an honorable retirement, with his full salary until his death."

Kanita hurt in her heart that she could not restore her father's position. That was an act against her father she could never fix or atone for. But at least she was able to do something for him in saving his reputation and his income.

"What else?" the king asked.

Kanita shrugged and shook her head. "Nothing," she said. "I only want to go home."

The king took her face in his hands and drew her to him. He kissed her forehead. "Then home is where you shall go," he said upon releasing her. "But first, stay, as my honored guest. Rest, bathe, eat." He clapped his hands and several servants rushed forward and took Kanita by the hand, leading her away, and Safi followed.

"Father," she heard Mongkut say. "I need to speak to you about Decha."

Kanita smiled to herself, proud that Mongkut had not lost his nerve.

CHAPTER NINETEEN

A few days later, Kanita and Safi were walking through one of the palace's many exquisite gardens when Mongkut caught up with them. They hadn't seen each other for several days, and Kanita hardly recognized him now in clean clothes and his hair sleekly tied upon his head.

"Hello, stranger," Kanita said with a warm smile, and Safi trumpeted a greeting. Kanita then remembered that she was talking to a prince, so she folded her hands in front of her and bowed.

"You don't have to do that," Mongkut said with a blush. He touched her arm to bring her back up.

"I do," she said, her eyes glancing around. "Someone is always watching in this place."

Mongkut nodded and then motioned back down the path Kanita had been walking on for them to continue, and Safi followed.

"I'm sorry I have been so busy since our return," Mongkut said.

"You are fine," Kanita said. "Your mother and the king's other wives have been spoiling me. I have never had so many baths in my life." She had actually never had a bath, not the way the king's women did, in a tub, with so many fragrant soaps and oils. She usually just washed in the river. They had also perfumed her hair and brushed it a thousand times. They gave her clothes of the softest silks. She felt like a princess. She knew she probably looked completely different from the wild jungle girl Mongkut had first met, but he was too polite to say anything.

"My mother is very taken with you," Mongkut said. "As is my father."

Something about Mongkut's tone made her pause. "What do you mean by that?" she asked.

"My father inquired as to your suitability as a wife to add to his harem," the prince said.

Kanita froze and could hardly form any words. "Wh-wh-wha—"

"But I told him you were already married," the prince went on.

Kanita gasped. "Oh no!" she cried.

"But that you were a widow," the prince said.

Kanita's head was spinning. She turned away from the prince and rubbed her face. "Why did you say those things?" she asked.

"Do you want to marry my father?" Mongkut asked.

"No!" Kanita said, aghast. "You know what I went through! I don't wish to marry at all. I had hoped when I got home, people would just think that Chakri had died in the jungle but never found me. I wanted a fresh start."

"Exactly!" Mongkut said. "If you went back and no one knew about Chakri, you would be free of him, but you could be forced to marry again before you were ready. This way, not only will your parents not be able to marry you off, you won't need a husband. If you ever marry, it will be because you want to."

"What do you mean?" Kanita asked, still a little confused.

"As Chakri's wife," Mongkut explained, "you're his heir! His money, his house, his property, it's all yours!"

Kanita's hand flew to her mouth. He was right. She had no idea how rich Chakri was, but she was sure he had more money than her family ever did. She could use the money to help support her parents so they wouldn't feel a need to marry her off and she could use it to support Safi so she would never be a burden.

She flew to the prince and hugged him, but only very quickly in case anyone saw her. She stood back with her hands over her heart.

"Thank you, Mongkut," she said. "But that was very mean, teasing me that your father wanted to marry me!"

"Oh, I wasn't kidding about that," Mongkut said. "He's married women younger than you before, and you are famous. Everyone in Bangkok is talking about you. You would have been a pretty jewel to put in his box. But we royals can't marry widows, so you are safe."

"Even though Chakri and I..." she asked, "...didn't consummate the marriage?"

"I told them the marriage was official," he said. "That I was forced to perform the ceremony. They didn't ask further details."

Kanita nodded and sighed in relief. With the prince himself reporting the marriage, no one would ever question its validity.

They turned and started walking again.

"What about Decha?" Kanita asked. She had been so curious about Decha's rebellion that she had asked the queen all about it. Of course, the queen was little more than the king's chief bedmate. She was not a queen in the sense that she had any ruling responsibilities. But she was well educated and read the newspapers often, so she knew quite a bit more about the history of Vientiane and Laos than Kanita ever did. So, while Kanita had learned more about the loss of the Vientiane kingdom, she had no idea what the king was planning to do about Decha since her return.

The prince sighed. "It is difficult to say what will happen. We cannot simply break the treaty with France without dire consequences. But my father admits the treaty was unfair. Unequal. He has agreed to at least meet with Decha, as opposed to having him shot on sight."

Kanita shook her head at the absurdity of it all. "Well, that is a slight improvement, I suppose."

"If the talks happen, Decha will at least have me on his side," the prince said with pride.

"That must have surprised your father," Kanita said. "For you to take up the cause of the men who kidnapped you."

"It did," Mongkut said. "But I think it is also what opened his eyes. If even I could be sympathetic to Decha's cause, then something must be done."

As they turned down another garden path, Safi reached out and pulled some beautiful purple flowers out of the ground and stuffed them into her mouth.

"Oh no, Safi!" Kanita said, and Mongkut laughed.

"So, what is next for you and Safi?" Mongkut asked. "I was surprised you are still here. I thought you would be excited to go home."

A Girl and Her Elephant 153

"I am...and I am not," Kanita said. "The king went ahead and sent an emissary to them with the good news about Safi being pardoned and my father being given an honorable retirement. I wanted to give them the good news myself, but there was no reason to leave them in anguish waiting for my return. So there has been no reason for me to rush back."

"But your parents, your home," Mongkut said. "Do you not miss it?"

Kanita paused and wrung her hands before asking a question she wasn't sure she wanted the answer to.

"Do you think my father will ever forgive me for the things I did?" she asked, her eyebrows raised in hopefulness.

Mongkut shrugged. "What if he doesn't?"

Kanita gasped and playfully slapped his arm. "That's not what you were supposed to say!"

"Well, it's a good question, right?" Mongkut insisted. "If you knew that your father was *never* going to forgive you, would you still go back?"

At first, she was shocked at his question, but then she gave the answer he knew she would give.

"Of course I would go back," Kanita said. "I miss my mother, and I worry about her. And I will spend the rest of my life trying to earn my father's forgiveness if I have to."

"Then that is your answer," Mongkut said.

Safi reached over and patted Kanita on the head.

"All right," Kanita said to Safi. "Let's go pack our things and head home."

Kanita climbed up on Safi's back and turned her toward the inner court where she had been staying.

"You're leaving?" Mongkut asked. "Just like that?"

"Just like that," Kanita said. She was anxious to get home. She had no idea what kind of greeting she would receive, but it didn't matter. She had Safi, so she had hope the future could still be bright.

The End

THANK YOU

Thank you for reading A Girl and Her Elephant! If you enjoyed it, I hope you will leave a review. If you want to know when the next Animal Companions adventure is released, be sure to join my mailing list!
http://zoeygong.com/subscribe/

A GIRL AND HER PANDA

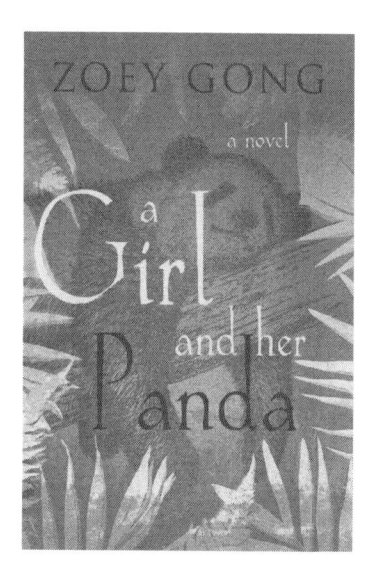

books2read.com/pandagirl

Lihua never could have imagined that the birth of a little brother would end the life she knew.

Raised in a poor country village, Lihua prayed her parents would have a son to bring peace and balance to the family. But she did not foresee how living in such poverty would force her parents to face a terrible choice they once made that would now cost Lihua everything.

Suddenly told to leave her home, Lihua begins a treacherous journey alone. After being attacked on the road the first day, an unlikely hero comes to her aid: a panda she decides to call Panpan. Bound together for love and survival, Lihua and Panpan travel together through the mountains and forest of western China as Lihua struggles to find her new place in the world.

A GIRL AND HER TIGER

books2read.com/tigergirl

She didn't plan on becoming a rebel...

After watching her parents serve in British households for her whole life, Priya had grown to despise every aspect of British colonialism. After an introduction to a British family in an attempt to secure a servant position of her own ends in disaster, Priya runs away to try and find a better life.

But she doesn't get far.

Alone on the streets of Bombay, Priya is kidnapped and taken captive aboard a smuggler's ship bound for the slave markets of the Americas.

And in the cage next to her – is a ferocious mama tiger named Nabhitha!

When Priya and the tiger see a chance for escape, will Priya dare to take it? Or will she end up the tiger's dinner?

Follow Priya and Nabhitha on a journey of courage and second chances.

ABOUT THE AUTHOR

ZOEY GONG was born and raised in rural Hunan Province, China. She has been studying English and working as a translator since she was sixteen years old. Now in her early twenties, Zoey loves traveling and eating noodles for every meal. She lives in Shenzhen with her cat, Jello, and dreams of one day disappointing her parents by being a Leftover Woman (剩女). Learn more at ZoeyGong.com.

- facebook.com/ZoeyGongAuthor
- goodreads.com/zoeygong
- bookbub.com/authors/zoey-gong

ABOUT THE PUBLISHER

*VISIT OUR WEBSITE
TO SEE ALL OF OUR HIGH QUALITY BOOKS:*

http://www.redempresspublishing.com

Quality trade paperbacks, downloads, audiobooks, and books in foreign languages in genres such as historical, romance, mystery, and fantasy.

Made in the USA
Monee, IL
04 September 2023